Threads

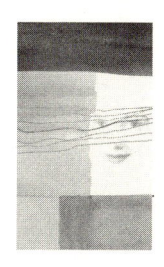

Patrice St. Onge

RED CANYON INK
GRAND JUNCTION, COLORADO

Threads

Copyright © 2006 Patrice Rowe

AUTHOR'S NOTE

This book is not about any particular people or places. This is a work of fiction. Names, characters, places and events are either products of the author's imagination or are intended to represent a fictional piece. Any resemblance to real people, living or dead, places or events is coincidental.

All rights reserved.
This book may not be duplicated, copied, transmitted or reproduced in any manner or by any means—electronic, mechanical, photographic, or optical, including methods not invented or in common use at the time of this publication—without the express written consent of the publisher.

Lyric excerpts for the following reprinted with permission:

Annie's Song
  Words and music by John Denver
  Copyright © 1974; renewed 2002 Anna Kate Deutschendorf, Zachary
    Deutschendorf and Jesse Belle Denver for the U.S.A.
  All rights for Anna Kate Deutschendorf and Zachary Deutschendorf administered
    by Cherry Lane Music Publishing Company, Inc. (ASCAP)
  All rights for Jesse Belle Denver administered by WB Music Corp. (ASCAP)
  International copyright secured. All rights reserved.

For You
  Words and music by John Denver
  Copyright © 1988 Cherry Mountain Music (ASCAP) and Dimensional Music Of
    109 (ASCAP)
  Worldwide rights for Cherry Mountain Music and Dimensional Music Of 1091
    administered by Cherry Lane Music Publishing Company, Inc.
  International copyright secured. All rights reserved.

PUBLISHED BY

Red Canyon Ink
2500 Broadway, Unit B, #235
Grand Junction, CO 81503
www.redcanyonink.com

Cover Design by David Rowe
Book Design and Production, Boulder Bookworks, Boulder, CO

ISBN 0-9772437-0-2
Library of Congress Control Number: 2005907421

Printed in the United States of America

For Farran and David

One is of my body,

one is of my soul,

both are in my heart—

thank you for the courage

to follow my dream.

Prologue

Jerry Searles puts it well:

> "People, like so many human shuttles,
> move in and out of each other's lives,
> mindlessly weaving the fabric of existence.
> Many are empty, with no fiber to trace
> their passing, while others leave some
> characteristic mark: a strand of tight-
> woven strength, a flash of color,
> perhaps some brief moment of contrast
> or eye-arresting pattern—not to mention,
> of course, the inevitable knots, snarls,
> flaws and monotonous disharmonies."

Interlude I

How do we become that which we are?

WHO IS THIS PERSON INHABITING MY BODY? *Maggie wonders. She feels like she is floating, detached from her physical body, standing in the grass below. She had tried astral projection in her hippie days when she was studying astrology and other paranormal phenomena. Now she is actually doing it without trying, no chanting or trance necessary. She stares at the gathered crowd. She wants to remember, remember the tastes, smells, touches, colors, faces… and the love pouring forth from friends, family, children and the sensations of losing and finding, finding and losing, losing, losing until, when all was lost, she found herself. That it takes all of this to reach yourself is her truth.*

How does one come to accept love after a lifetime of yearning for it, running from it, having it slip through your fingers, holding its tiny body, seeing it masquerading, masked, deceitful, watching it offered and withdrawn, standing as they lowered it into the ground, crying from the pain of it, feeling it against your skin, warm, shivering at its loss, shedding pounds at its disappearance, and then…

black and blue

You gave me life and bad lungs no one knew the effects of secondhand smoke back then; I knew right from wrong: you were always right, I was always wrong; I worked hard, too hard, and worried too much because you forgot we were children and not small adults; you tried with limited skills to do the right things, succeeding sporadically; there were other types of parents, I know, because my friends had them; I loved and hated you, you never asked forgiveness and I never gave it until the poison chained me to your path; I learned to let go and became free, free to be the person I was born to be; after emerging, I learned to lead with courage and ask forgiveness; I learned that conflict is not bad and that talking things out is important, rather than slamming doors and silence; in your defense, you had no role model, so you were no role model, just tried to get by each day; I judge you by my reality and realize yours was quite different, that I judge you at all, I learned, is not your truth, it is that your sadness and confusion never saw the light; it took me years to see and accept that you were flawed and beautiful for it, I neither hide from it nor curse it, but seek to understand it and laugh with my belly shaking at the absurdity of the human condition.

JOHN SITS IN THE WAITING ROOM of St Joseph's Hospital; number five is on the way. He rubs the stubble on his chin as he remembers the joy of his first born, a son, and sort of remembers the three others, each birth becoming less distinct from the previous one. They just seem to keep coming. He is there so often he is surprised the hospital does not charge him rent.

The smell is always the same: Pine Sol, bleach and something he cannot identify. It's death. It lurks in the hallways waiting for the opportunity to collect souls too loosely connected to this world. The walls are institutional green, the color of his boyhood schoolrooms. Only in the hospital, the walls do not have that layer of gray dirt. His mother and mother-in-law are in the waiting room, too, along with a brother and sister or two. He wonders why his mother has come. She hates his wife and detests the fact they keep bringing more children into the world. She is a large woman who fancies exotic hats and wears her mink stole, even in the middle of the heat and humidity of August. John cannot remember his mother ever smiling or cracking a joke. Life is serious business to her. Never a quiet woman, she has made her opinion known about his wife. He has heard her use the word hussy when referring to Mary Ann.

There is a lot of commotion in the hall and several doctors rush into the delivery room. Twenty, thirty minutes pass; John stands and stretches.

"Does anyone want anything? I'm making a cafeteria run."

"Yeah, I'll take a Coke. Never mind, I'll come with," his brother Chuck says. Chuck is the crazy bachelor brother who paints houses for a living and loses most of his pay to his poker buddies. Consequently, he is a beloved companion. He has a well-developed sense of humor in spite of, or maybe because of, the surroundings and influences of his childhood.

His brother jokes on the way to the cafeteria, "Hey, I like my cigar but I take it out of my mouth once in awhile." His quote of a

Groucho Marx comment brings a smile to John's face. "What number is this anyway?" he asks.

John knows he knows it's number five but he humors him. "It's number twenty-seven, but who's counting? I figure I can start a major league baseball team soon."

Just as they get back, drinks in hand, a physician in green scrubs approaches. "Mr. Casey?"

"Yes, I'm Mr. Casey," John replies.

"Well, it's a girl. Your wife is doing fine, but the baby is having some breathing problems, so we're watching her closely. She's on oxygen, but you may see her."

John puts out his cigarette and follows the doctor into the nursery. Blue eyes framed by dark hair peer up at him from around the oxygen mask, her little chest heaving rapidly; a tiny indentation appears with each rattling inhale. He holds her; she has no weight. Head to toe, she barely goes beyond his outstretched fingers. He is never quite sure what to do with them when they are this size. "Is she supposed to be this color?" he asks the nurse.

"Well, she does have a respiratory problem, but we think it will take care of itself. We'll keep a close watch on her."

He hands the baby back to the nurse and goes to see his wife.

MARY ANN IS EXHAUSTED from ten hours of labor and the epidural left her with an excruciating headache. She cringes at the sight of her husband.

He bends down to kiss her but she turns her head.

"The baby is beautiful," he tries. Mary Ann does not move. "I'm sure her breathing will get better, she seems real strong."

Mary Ann continues to stare out the window. "Have you seen her? Maybe they could bring her in," John suggests. When no response is forthcoming, he turns to leave. "Your ma is in the waiting room, I'll send her in."

In the waiting room he shares the news. "The baby will be fine, just a little breathing problem." He sends Mary's mom in to see her. The rest of them walk to the nursery window to look at his latest arrival. After the usual comments about who she looks like and some good-natured ribbing, his relatives congratulate him and leave.

His mother frowns and says, "the child looks scrawny. I told you she doesn't eat right."

John holds his breath and his tongue, willing his blood pressure to return to normal.

"I hope you have a good Catholic name picked out for her," is his mother's parting shot. He does, he thinks, Margaret Mary Casey.

Alone, he looks at his watch, 11:15 p.m. A wave of exhaustion washes over him with the realization of the time and the fact he has one more mouth to feed. He lights another cigarette off the butt of the previous one and then stubs it out. His paycheck from the factory already does not stretch to cover the cost of the other four, but he figures they will manage. Maybe he will get that promotion or maybe he can pick up some side work stacking bricks at the brickyard. They are always looking for extra laborers.

Hell, it is 1951 and the world is changing fast. He just read about some kind of new bomb called a hydrogen bomb and Dr. Salk found a vaccine for polio. Some other scientists found something they called DNA. It's like the Sears and Roebuck Catalog of the body. We'll probably be able to pick the eye and hair color of our next kid, he thinks. There must be something he can do to make more money. A second job would not be so bad. He can see that American Dream, dangling out there like the proverbial carrot, and is willing to do what it takes to chase it. Besides he does not mind getting away from Mary Ann's nagging. Someday she will see a successful man standing in front of her and be proud.

John slips back into Mary Ann's room to say good night. She is asleep so he tiptoes out and goes home. He remembers a different Mary Ann, one who was the life of the party and the best-looking wife of the bunch. She will be fine. She just needs some rest and she will be her old self. But he knows it is a lie as soon as he thinks it.

Back at home John falls into an exhausted sleep on the couch. He dreams he is a Big Band leader like Glenn Miller, up in the spotlight. The crowd goes wild as they wrap up another evening at the Starlight Ballroom. He heads backstage to his dressing room. Women swarm around him for autographs and he accommodates them with delight. In his dressing room are bottles of champagne and tins of caviar. A valet takes his jacket and hangs it up, but, in the back of the closet, he sees a child with dark eyes staring back at him struggling to breathe.

In the middle of the night a nurse calls for assistance: the little girl Casey is blue when she checks on her. They manually ventilate her and she revives. John and Mary Ann never know.

John's sweaty body bolts upright, almost falling off the couch. He rubs his eyes until they focus on the blue haze of the TV set, its off-the-air symbol staring back at him. He stumbles upstairs to bed and falls back into a fitful sleep. At 5:30 A.M. he brings his fist down on the button of the alarm clock and shuffles to the shower. An hour later he is on the train, heading to the tire factory where he is floor foreman of the injection mold division.

That evening with Mary Ann still in the hospital, John makes grilled cheese sandwiches for his four children. With the friction between him and Mary Ann absent, he relaxes and jokes with the kids. It's a rare event and he is enjoying it. Like all 1950's dads he wants more for his children and he wants more for himself. He wants his children to love him. His cold, sterile childhood with his severe mother and emotionally absent father left a black hole that he wants so badly to fill. Once his music, Mary Ann, at least at the beginning of their relationship, and then one child after another all were attempts to fill in the gap in his soul. Maybe that's why all those babies keep coming. The hole just seems bottomless, though.

After dinner his seven year old daughter, Jackie, crawls in his lap and asks him to read a book. He wraps his arms around her and feels the hole close just a bit.

A week later Mary Ann and John take their new baby girl home, but, within a month, she is back in the hospital with pneumonia. A week and a lot of antibiotics later, she is sent home again. This would be one of many cycles that would repeat throughout her life.

Through the next several years, they take turns going to family functions. Someone must stay home with the almost always ailing baby girl Casey. Mary Ann does not mind; it provides her with an excuse to avoid her mother-in-law.

John fell in love with all the pieces of Mary Ann. It wasn't just her looks that attracted him; it was the sense of excitement that vibrated around her. She was daring and made him want to break out. Break out of the coffin-like mold he was raised in. He wanted to pour his soul out through his horn and let the sweet notes carry him to the edge of the universe. A loud horn blast interrupts his thoughts as the assembly line comes to a dead stop. He grabs a large wrench and loosens the jammed bolts, realigns them and flips the switch, the conveyor belt creeks into motion. Fifteen more minutes and it's quitting time. A moment of elation and then reality sets in. The hour train ride home gives him time to prepare himself, but for what? He dreads opening the door. How the hell did they get like this? Mary Ann will be into her third drink, her eyes will overflow with disgust and disappointment. He can take the disgust but he hates to see the disappointment. He hates more that he tries to defeat it with his fists. Sometimes it's her, sometimes one of his children. In the moments after he sobs. As the train approaches the station, dread expands in his chest.

The stress of the doctor bills mount, only to be eased by a cold beer or two, or three, with Mary Ann when he arrives home each night. That's when the fight starts. Mary Ann's inebriated state loosens her tongue. "You're a loser, a lousy factory-working loser. I could have had any number of men, men who became something, but no, I chose the south-side loser. Look at you; look at your gut hanging over your pants. You can't even see your feet. You disgust me." The harangue goes on for hours. Finally, John can take no more so he heads uptairs to bed. He hears coughing from down the hall as he switches off the light.

Each winter the Casey girl coughs nonstop until the spring thaw soothes her ravaged lungs. After she starts school, she is embarrassed by the need to be sent out of the classroom to get a drink of water, even though it does nothing to quiet the rattle in her chest. Her parents can not afford the prescription medication she needs so they douse her with cough syrup and send her to school with Luden's cough drops, but the bronchitis is much more stubborn than over-the-counter remedies. Teachers reprimand her for disturbing the class. She holds her breath, trying to stop the hacking, but nothing works so she endures being chastised.

Winter is not the only problem season. Summer brings allergies and asthma. In spite of the afflictions, or maybe to compensate for them, she plays rough and tumble with the boys, striving to be the strongest and the fastest. Most days after school find Maggie out with playmates, fighting bad guys, climbing trees or building roads with Tonka Trucks in the dirt hills. Most of all, she loves the dirt, it is real, honest and clean.

Interlude II

They rise early before the hoards in the house and sneak out, each with a small hidden parcel. The truck climbs the long hill to their favorite place overlooking an incredible montage of colored dirt—red, yellow, burnt sienna, raw umber. Canyon walls rise and fall from view. Chilled morning air awakens their lungs and nostrils to the intricacies of the desert at dawn. He pulls the truck to a halt in front of a large boulder. She grabs some tissue before exiting the truck. A large outcropping provides their amphitheater-like seating. They sit on the edge and snuggle for a moment, acknowledging the Great Spirit's brisk announcement of the day, smelling the heat that will grace the afternoon as it hovers just beyond the horizon.

    Maggie pulls a box from under her fleece jacket and hands it to David. He opens it, removing the tape without tearing the paper. Inside is a pocket watch inscribed with the date and a message: "My love for you is timeless." Tears run into the creases of his grizzled cheeks. "Thank you, it's beautiful" is all he can will his voice to say. She hands him a tissue. After opening and closing the clasp several times, he wraps her in his arms while silent tears drop onto her shoulder.

He regains his composure and proffers a small box from his pocket. Maggie pulls the tape and paper off in one swift motion. Inside the velvet box is an abstract silver and copper heart necklace also inscribed with the date. He helps her put it on and wipes her tears. "I love you, I love you, I love you" he keeps repeating. Maggie crawls deeper into his embrace and listens to his beating heart which she now wears around her neck.

2

blue

You let me skip school to shop with you, I liked that about you, you drank away the mortgage, I did not like that; you were unhappy in a time where such things were hidden, we suffered in the closet with you; your jekyll and hyde personality scared me, I never knew who would meet me at the door; I stayed away a lot and I never brought friends home or had sleepovers; I did not know your demons, maybe if I had I would have had more compassion; I sensed that your life turned out much differently than you planned in your seventeen-year-old head; jealousy kept our father at bay, wanted him for yourself, craved the attention but it was never enough; was it just diseased genes or did a life of financial struggle, low self-esteem and broken dreams kill your will to live; I carry some of your traits, some good, most not; I do not sweat the small stuff but I had to learn to not need the limelight, to not be the center of the universe; from you I learned a lot of what not to do and a little of what to do.

At five feet seven, Mary Ann draws attention. She is curvaceous, which was desirable at the time, with dark hair, eyes, and full lips long before the collagen craze. She is considered pretty hot stuff. Men jockey for a chance to dance with her at the USO. All those handsome faces in dress uniform make her knees weak. They represent the world outside her ethnic neighborhood. Many of them have just come home from Europe, full of stories of Paris—its food, wine and sophistication. She dreams of dancing on the Champs-Elysees till dawn with some good-looking naval officer. Max, the short-order cook shouts "orders up" and her dream is interrupted by eggs over easy and hash browns. She pours coffee by the gallon and tolerates local boys' advances.

On Saturday night she and her sister plan to go to the Starlight Ballroom. The Great Lakes Naval Base is supplying the evening's selection and she plans to get the most handsome one. They have to sneak out; their mother would die if she knew they were dancing with sailors. They are not even allowed to go to picture shows without a chaperone. Mary Ann thinks of her mother as a dolt and a pushover. She is used to getting her way except when it comes to interfacing with the outside world. Sneaking out is not a problem; her mother goes to bed by eight-thirty each evening.

Mary Ann surveys the crowd while her sister Jane gets them each a glass of punch. Lots of faces but none strike her fancy. The band hits the first note of "Boogie Woogie Bugle Boy" and the dance floor is flooded with dress whites. Mary Ann feels her hand being tugged and joins a short redheaded boy on the dance floor. As the band hits the last note, she excuses herself to go find Jane.

After a few songs the bandleader introduces a young sailor who can "really wail on the horn." A dark-haired young man around six foot tall, in dress whites, jumps up on the stage, grabs the trumpet being handed to him and joins the band in a rousing rendition of "Bumble Boogie."

Mary Ann turns from her conversation with Jane to check out the band. Jane continues to talk to her, "Mar, Mar, hey, snap out of it."

"Huh, what?" is Mary Ann's distant response. Mary Ann does not take her eyes off the stage.

Jane follows her gaze. "Hey, he's a looker, not bad on the horn either."

As the music ends, the bandleader hollers out, "Let's give a big hand to John Casey." Mary Ann is already making her way to the stage.

MARY ANN FELL IN LOVE with a jazz trumpet player and married an assembly-line worker. They are one in the same; she just could not know it at seventeen. She loves the lives of the rich and famous and lives the life of the poor and obscure. When attempts to seduce herself into a more glamorous life fail, she lives vicariously through stars on the screen and liquor. A vague longing she has no vocabulary for gnaws at her. The sixties haven't liberated women, yet. She is caught in between her mother's generation who ironed everything, even men's boxer shorts, and a generation of women who will operate backhoes. Her Irish-Catholic upbringing produces offspring who confound her. She is supposed to feel some attachment—something inside, but there is no room within her. Her fears, insecurity, vanity and naïveté consume her. Women of her time do not have Prozac; they have men, movies and alcohol; she disappears into them all.

Mary Ann looks over at John's protruding midsection and feels like running, out the door, down the street, across the town, until she finds something new. She is not sure what. Instead she finishes brushing the hair of her fifth-born child and sends her off to bed. She gets up and pours a drink.

The next morning Mary Ann sits at the kitchen table, a cup of coffee and a cigarette for breakfast. She props her swollen ankles up on an adjacent chair. An eighth child, Jesus! Why had they not stopped years ago? Even though she is Irish, she is hardly Catholic. Given the choice between sleeping in on Sunday morning and Mass she chooses the former. Her husband, however, is devoted to his church and rounds up the brood each Sunday for Mass at St. Xavier's. As the children grow they attend the Mass based on altar boy and choir schedules and are happy to no longer attend with their father and receive the evil eye and vise grip on the shoulder should their concentration stray.

Mary Ann is an EC—Easter and Christmas Catholic. She loves the chance to show off new styles and her ability to turn out seven, soon to be eight, clean and shiny offspring as a tribute to her own perception of great mothering skills. It is also an opportunity to confront the stares of the Country Club, Gardening Club, and Ladies Sodality, those holier-than-thou faces with secrets hidden in their white gloves and behind lace veils.

She pours another cup of coffee and feels another wave of nausea. It is not morning sickness, she is past that. What if he finds out? There are so many, will he even notice if one looks slightly different? Hell, they all look different; there's enough variation in the gene pool to have produced two hair colors and three eye colors already, so maybe this one will blend in.

Maggie, her blue-eyed middle daughter comes in, mopey face and suitcase in tow. Now what? This is the dramatic one, always emotional and demanding attention. She cringes as the youngster approaches.

"I'm running away," she declares. "No one here likes me. I'm sick of all these hand-me-down clothes and the kids at school making fun of me and I hate sleeping with my brother who still wets the bed and you yelled at me for something Judy did." She watches as her six-year-old picks up her suitcase and struggles down the steep stairs.

"Wait a minute," Mary Ann calls after her.

Good! The young girl thinks, maybe my mom is sorry and will buy me some new clothes. Her mother meets her at the bottom of the stairs.

"Open your suitcase," she demands. The stairway stinks of garbage and stale beer from the stacks of bottles in the corner. The dark-haired child stares up, not comprehending.

"Open your suitcase," her mother repeats.

She sets the case down and snaps open the latches. There on top of her t-shirts and shorts is her favorite doll. Her mother reaches down and snatches it up. "You can't take anything with you that I bought, so this doll will have to stay." Her mother turns and marches upstairs, holding her back with the doll flopping around by one arm. The little girl looks up with tears ready to spill. How cruel, how can she run away without Sophie? It would be like abandoning her baby. After closing her suitcase, she opens the door and steps out onto the front stoop. The sadness crumples her legs so she sits down and cries into her hands. The row of houses with peeling paint stare at the little girl, eyes watch from upstairs windows. This neighborhood is used to commotion at this residence, it happens often. Moments later her friend Ellie sits down next to her and asks what is wrong. She repeats what happened. Ellie agrees that her mom is mean and then asks if she wants to play hopscotch.

"Yeah, I guess so," she says as she wipes her nose on her sleeve.

LATER THAT DAY, Mary Ann's sister Jane stops by with her four children. The girls race to the bedroom to play. Her thirteen-year-old daughter, Judy, and her age-matched cousin Diane lie on the bed and peel wallpaper while discussing boys and what to do next. "I got an idea," Diane says. "You got a robe?"

The houses are so close they can smell what the neighbors are having each meal. Lots of polish sausage in this neighborhood. The bousha and za-za (Polish for grandma and grandpa, respectively) wage a daily war with keeping the hoodlums next door off their lawn. Za-za hides in the bushes at night and chases them off with his cane. The teenage Caseys and their friends run just around the corner of the house and collapse in laughter.

Judy finds a sash off a robe and they set to work. It takes the two of them to push open the rain-swollen window. Two-stories down is the forbidden lawn. They slide something through the opening and lower it with the sash. A moment later there is a pounding at the bedroom door and Mary Ann bursts in. "What the hell are you doing?" the frantic mother screams. Pull her in now!" The two teens whirl around to face the outraged mother. In their panic they let go of the sash. Mary Ann screams again. She stares in shock. "What have you done to your sister?" The two girls erupt in laugher. Mary Ann does not comprehend the situation and runs to the window. There on the ground she sees the lifelike Patty Play Pal doll and a wave of relief and then anger washes over her, one after another. She turns on the girls and levels her gaze.

"You're grounded for two weeks, missy. Don't you ever pull a stunt like that again. You scared the daylights out of the Wisniewskis next door. Your mother can deal with you," she says as she turns to address her niece. "Now get downstairs and get that doll and then you can just stay in this room for the rest of the day."

After retrieving the doll, the two girls roll around on the bed in silent laughter. It worked; the neighbors thought they were hanging her six-year-old sister out the window. So what if they scared the old coots. It served them right for being so nosy. It was well worth the two-week grounding to know they had gotten to the busybodies.

Maggie enters the bedroom suitcase in hand.

"What's so funny?"

Judy and Diane alternate telling the story of hanging the doll out the window and how her mother went berserk when she thought it was the six-year-old and not the doll.

"Mom was really mad when she thought it was me?" asks the six-year-old.

"Yeah, she just blew a gasket" was her older sister's reply.

The six-year-old thought back to the scene on the stairs and wrinkled her forehead.

Outside on the playground on Monday morning, Judy repeats the story to her friend Paulette, who laughs until tears roll down her cheeks.

3

goldenrod

Our protector against the bullies on the block, your mom served lemonade and cookies on hot afternoons, you swam in our back porch pool; from you I learned my first lesson about true friends, one that I would have to relearn from time to time, I also learned the power of peer pressure and the need to resist it.

THEY SQUARE OFF IN THE MIDDLE OF THE STREET in a small town indistinct from any other small town in the Midwest. A crowd gathers around, encouraging them. Robby, blond hair slicked back into a wave, blue jeans cuffed, circles, hands held up in front of his face like his dad showed him. His blue eyes watch from between the boxing gloves. The big kids put them up to it. He and his best friend had been arguing over Tonka Trucks, who would get which one. Robby wanted the dump truck and so did his friend. A few more neighborhood kids stop to watch. The August heat and humidity cling to them. White-bread kids in rolled up blue jeans and t-shirts sweat in the noonday sun. The rows of identical brick houses shimmer in the heat rising off asphalt driveways. Mothers make lemonade and stand in the kitchen in front of the fan, arm flesh dangling as they cool themselves with hair piled on heads.

Back in the street the two combatants continue to circle.

"C'mon, throw a punch, don't just dance around."

"Yeah, hit 'im," taunts a red-haired boy. "What are you chicken? *bauk, bauk!*"

But still they just circle, scared eyes peering out between oversized gloves, their skinny, scrawny arms struggling to hold them up. Why are they fighting? Robby wonders. This is his best friend; he does not want to hurt anyone. The crowd's patience decreases with the increase in heat as the chant "Punch 'im", grows in volume and urgency. Robby turns to look at the big kids; he is six and they are twelve, maybe thirteen. What should he do? As he turns back, he sees a flash, and then blood and pain follow. He is on the ground, holding his nose as blood runs down his arm. His best friend is staring, shocked at the outcome. Maggie did not mean to hurt him. She just could not take the big kids yelling and yelling to punch him. She wanted them to shut up. The crowd was silent now. Several kids help Robby up and take him home.

"What'd do that for?"

"Yeah, ya didn't have to hurt him," shouts another voice.

The crowd turns their back on her and walks away. One girl remains.

"I'll still be your friend," Suzie says.

Suzie helps her remove the boxing gloves and wipes the tears and sweat from her face.

"Would you like some lemonade?" she asks.

"Sure," sniffles the little girl.

Arm in arm they walk to Suzie's house; Suzie's just pre-teen body towering over the first-grader.

From Suzie's front porch she can hear her mother calling her.

"I'd better go. Thank you for the lemonade and for being my friend. Can we play tomorrow?"

"Sure, I'll come by and get you."

"Bye."

4

green

A loof, no one really knew who you were, you wanted it that way, you gave the illusion of friendship, never the real thing; I wanted to be like you but then grew into myself and am much better for it.

HER MOTHER YANKS HARDER ON HER HAIR in an effort to still her while she finishes the last braid. Lorraine holds still for a moment and then begins shifting from foot to foot.

"If you don't hold still you'll be late for school," her mother scolds.

Her sister Paulette calls up stairs, "It's time to go, hurry up; I don't want to be late."

Soon two well-heeled blond girls walk down the street, exact same uniforms and hair bows. Their stomachs are full along with their lunch boxes. Their starched white blouses and teeth glow in the sunlight. As they near the school, friends join in the journey. Paulette tells Lorraine to join her own friends—it's embarrassing to have a younger sister tagging along now that she is in junior high.

St. Xavier's playground is alive with motion and noise. Lorraine is playing with a dark-haired girl, whose hair seems to be on a journey of its own into the unknown, strands reaching out in all directions. Her face is a little dirty and her uniform probably dou-

21

bled as pajamas. They join in a game of Farmer in the Dell. Soon the bell rings, summoning them to their classroom.

After school, Lorraine's friend begs to come over and play. Lorraine says "Sure" and off they go, hand in hand, skipping to a song they learned in music class.

Mrs. Rasmussen cringes as her daughter enters the house.

"Oh Lorraine, can I see you in your bedroom for a moment?"

"Sure, Mom," came the reply. She turned to her friend. "Wait here, I'll be right back."

"Lorraine, I thought I told you not to bring friends home without asking."

"I know, Mom, but we just want to play a little while."

"Well, you know this girl is not...." Her mother stops to search for the right words. "Not like us."

"What do you mean?" Lorraine asks.

"Well, um, she's Irish and they're different. Her parents might not like her being here."

She felt clever for shifting the focus from herself. Lorraine just stared.

"So what do I tell her?"

"Just say you forgot you have a piano lesson so she has to go."

"But I don't have a piano lesson until tomorrow. Won't that be a lie?"

"That's okay, it's just a little white lie so that your friend doesn't get in trouble."

"Oh, okay." Her stomach feels queasy as she heads for the kitchen.

In the kitchen her friend stands nervously trying to tame her wayward hair. She bites at her dirty fingernails and surveys the room. Everything is white and clean. The house is devoid of the smell of corned beef and cabbage. There are no dirty dishes stacked in the sink or grubby fingerprints on the refrigerator. No stacks of mail and school papers cover the countertop. The stark cleanliness of the kitchen makes her stomach grumble; she remembers that she did not have lunch. There was nothing in the refrigerator this morning and her mom was still asleep. She did not dare wake her.

Mrs. Rasmussen enters the kitchen smiling. Lorraine enters with a strange look on her face.

"Sorry, we can't play today. I have a piano lesson."

Her friend's shoulders drop as she mumbles that it's okay, maybe they could play another day.

Mrs. Rasmussen chimed in brightly, "Oh, that's a wonderful idea."

On her way home from the rich neighborhood Maggie recounts the day. Today is Monday; Lorraine takes piano on Tuesdays. Oh well, maybe it changed, she thinks, as she crosses through the cemetery into her neighborhood.

Ellie, a friend of hers, sees her coming and waves from across the street, "Wanna play hopscotch?"

"Yep, I'll go get my chalk."

Interlude III

The salon is quiet this Saturday afternoon. Maggie glances over at her daughter, Grace, who has grown into a beautiful young woman. The stylist gently moves her head back to set another curl. The manicurist is talking away to Grace; she wonders what they are discussing. Maggie is next for the manicurist. The early afternoon is filled with hair, nails and make-up, in preparation.

The house is being transformed. She leans back in the chair and reflects on her own transformation.

5

baby blue

Y*ou lived with your dad; your parents were divorced, in the early 1960s, that made you different, your mom had a monkey for a pet, that made her weird and cool at the same time; we played jump rope and hula hoop by the hour, your dad made us peanut butter and mayonnaise sandwiches, I still eat them; I told stories and we turned them into plays, outside our family dramas we shared the innocence of childhood.*

ELLIE WATCHES AS HER DAD POUNDS A NAIL into the living room wall. He hangs the bracket that houses the curtain rod. Next he feeds the curtain, an old sheet, onto the curtain rod and slides it across the length of the rod.

"I'm going to make popcorn, Dad," she calls out as she walks to the kitchen.

"Okay, just don't burn yourself like the last time."

"I won't."

Ellie pulls out a blackened pot from the white enameled cupboard and places it on the gas burner. She adds the oil and waits for it to heat up. She puts in one kernel and waits for it to pop. When it does she adds two cups of corn and covers the pot. She shakes it over the fire to prevent burning. Soon the kernels are popping away like fireworks on the Fourth of July. Ellie shakes the pan until the popping subsides. She pours the freshly popped corn into a bowl and starts the process over. There are at least fifteen kids in the neighborhood who are either in the play or coming to see it. She supposes a few parents will come too. She continues to make popcorn until she has filled several large bowls. Next is the lemonade. Ellie makes four pitchers and hopes it will be enough.

Her next-door neighbor has written the play. It is about three kids stranded on a deserted island after the ship they are sailing on gets caught in a storm and crashes on some rocks. All the adults are killed and the three kids have to survive and figure out how to get back home. Ellie is playing one of the shipwrecked kids along with Joey Mancuso and Shelley Papineau. Her friend, the playwright, is directing the show. They are all nine to ten years old and love the make-believe part of being in a play. Each actor chooses his or her own wardrobe based on their own selection of clothing; they are going for a Robinson Crusoe look. They agree to cork their faces so they look dirty. Ellie's dad improvises scenery: a campfire, trees and beach. He spreads plastic sheeting and hauls sand from the backyard, cuts off tree branches and tacks them to the walls and makes cardboard flames for the fire. They collect all the folding chairs in the neighborhood for seating. A cardboard box turned upside down is the concession stand. Mary Kay Bracken will sell the refreshments and tickets. They are charging a quarter for admission. The proceeds will be used to fund their next venture.

As it nears two o'clock, the living room starts to fill. Popcorn and lemonade are scooped up for a nickel each. Ellie looks out from behind the sheet and is astonished at the number of kids and parents. They must be from other blocks because she does not recognize them all. The noise level rises as Mr. Collins, Ellie's dad, walks to center stage. The living room is packed. Parents sitting on child-size stools smile and begin to quiet the children around them. Mr. Collins, acting as narrator, sets the stage for the play and then Jimmy and Johnny Hawkins slide the sheet to the side. The play lasts forty minutes and ends to a rousing round of applause.

The cast and director take several bows and the sheet is closed. Lemonade pitchers and popcorn bowls are scraped bare. The crowd shuffles out, talking about how they would have saved the group if that had happened to them.

Skinny Lenny slams the screen door as he exits. "I'd a built a plane and flew out of there."

His twin, Louis one-ups him. "Yeah, well, I'd a made a telegraph to signal passing ships."

"It was cool how they made a raft and sailed to a nearby island and made friends with the natives who helped them flag down a ship to take them home," A third kid pops in.

The play is the talk of the block for the next week.

Ellie finishes counting the ticket and concession money. "We made ten dollars and twenty-five cents." The amount in 1961 dollars is astonishing to the ten year olds.

"Wow, we can probably buy a real curtain," Joey blurts out.

"Yeah, or maybe some costumes or paint for sets," are other responses from the cast. The group agrees to have Mr. Collins hold it until they decide how best to spend it. They all stay to help clean up. The playwright, Maggie, is already thinking about the next play, one with a mean stepmother who keeps kids locked up in a dungeon and how they escape and find a nice new mother.

It is a sad day in the neighborhood when the Casey family announces they will be moving to a town thirty or so miles away. Ellie hugs Maggie and vows to write to her and come visit, even though she has no sense of distances or directions. The neighborhood is going to be awfully quiet without the Casey clan.

6

grey

Yours was a class of order and reason, all things in their place including the children; you despised disorder, irregularities, and the skinny little girl in the third row, you showed her, didn't you, with your ruler and superior way; from you I learned low self-esteem and the skills to survive it.

SISTER MARY AGNES SCANS THE CLASSROOM; all the children sit erect with hands folded on their desks, as they should. All is in order except that new skinny girl in the third row. One of those Casey kids, she thinks. Which one is it again? Oh yeah, Margaret, she answers herself. Is she ever going to wear the right uniform? Navy jumper with school emblem, white blouse with Peter Pan collar, royal blue continental tie, and royal blue knee socks is the proper ensemble. This girl, however, is guilty of multiple offenses. Navy blue socks, blouses with pointed collars, some days she wears a dress, no uniform at all. Rules are there for a reason. It is the rules that drew her to the convent. Each day begins and ends the same; it is how she likes it. Her slovenly parents with their gypsy ways are long dead and she feels little remorse. Her God and her church are her family.

Sister Agnes began life as Josephine Bohakowitz, the sixth daughter of Julius and Irma. They immigrated to the United States from Bohemia in 1910 when Josephine was ten years old. The family wandered from New York, to Detroit and finally to Chicago doing whatever odd jobs would put food on the table. They supplemented with larceny. They worked the busy streets, lifting wallets and anything else not nailed down. Josephine hid out in local churches, praying for the souls of her family. She lit candle after candle asking the Blessed Virgin Mary to deliver her from her family. At thirteen she entered the convent of the Sacred Heart of Mary and had no further contact with her family. She missed her sister, Margaret, the only one to share her aversion to their lifestyle. It was a shame Margaret did not share her convocation. Josephine had tried to convince her to join the convent but Margaret dreamed of a husband and children so Josephine just prayed for her.

In October of 1920, Josephine became Sister Mary Agnes. She was overjoyed by the shedding of her past and purity of a future as God's bride.

Sister Agnes singles out the pathetic creature and orders her to the hallway. Every Monday starts like this. Classmates look on with sympathy and relief—sad it is her again; glad it is not them. The girl stands head down, staring at the scuffed toes of her shoes. The cardboard she put in the bottoms did not spare her socks. The hole grew so big she finally had to throw them out. Her parent's can not afford a second pair.

"Where are your royal blue socks?" Sister Agnes demands.

"I, I don't know," the girl stammers.

"What do you mean you don't know?"

"I, I couldn't find them this morning," is all she can think of to say. The truth would not have mattered anyway.

"Hold out your hands," Sister Agnes commands.

The girl does as she is told, flinching as the steel ruler strikes her knuckles repeatedly. After finishing the last stroke, Sister Agnes pauses, stunned by the thought of a sister she has not seen in forty years. Peculiar to think of her now. She recovers and admonishes the girl.

"Now you find those socks and wear them. Understand me?"

The girl just nods. Back in class she holds her eyes straight and stares holes in the chalkboard so she does not see the stares.

Every week Sister Agnes addresses the transgressors. Each Monday the girl finds herself back in the hallway, answering to a litany of sins.

"Why isn't your tuition paid? It's two months overdue. You take this note to your parents. Where is your tie? You're supposed to wear it everyday not just when you feel like it."

The truth is her brother and she share one tie and take turns wearing it. She listens to how God is not pleased with her for these lapses in responsibility, like a fourth grader knows why the tuition is not paid or how to acquire proper uniform items.

Another Sunday night rolls around and she realizes her mother has not done the laundry and she is too tired to put a load in at nine o'clock. She knows she will not have a clean uniform for the morning.

Monday comes and the girl's seat is empty. Out ill states the note she proffers the next day. Again Monday comes and no girl. Her note says she had a stomach ache. The next week she does not attend at all. Pneumonia lands her in the hospital. Sister Agnes is happy not to have to deal with her and her subliminally rebellious attitude. That little urchin has too much pride but Sister Agnes knows how to change that. When finally a Monday comes with the girl in attendance, the wrong blouse and no tuition send her to the cloakroom until lunch. In addition to the normal two hours of homework, she will now have to make up what she is missing in class but she likes the quiet and makes up stories in her head to pass the time. The hours drone by and she imagines a horrible fire breaking out in the school. Her lightning-fast reflexes save tens of students as she returns over and over to the burning building to pull them to safety. She considers leaving Sister Agnes but then visualizes her undying gratitude for saving her life. Sister Agnes makes her the favored student and even invites her to the convent for lunch, this being an event reserved for only the truly special few. There is an award banquet in her honor where she humbly accepts a plaque with her name engraved in gold.

Maggie wishes Ellie and her dad were there to turn the stories into plays. She misses Ellie and is sad that she will probably never see her again. The new school she is attending is meaner than her previous one. She likes her new house and there are lots of kids in her new neighborhood but she still wishes Ellie was here with her. She stares up at the window wishing she could open it. The smell of fifty years of lunches sometimes makes her nauseous. She can identify most of the smells: baloney, salami, peanut butter and jelly and an occasional hard-boiled egg. The hard-boiled eggs are the worst. They smell like someone just farted. She chuckles at the thought of rich kids farting in a proper parlor. The rich kids have the lunch boxes with cartoon characters on them, but mostly kids have brown paper bags with their names written on them in pencil, pen and sometimes crayon. They are all lined up on the shelf above the coat hooks. She longs for a lunch box but knows she is condemned to a brown bag unless they finally realize she is adopted and her real parents come to claim her and take her home to their mansion where she has beautiful clothes and a bedroom to herself.

The next Monday comes and her father calls up and down the hall for everyone to get up for school. Luke, her younger brother, hollers out that she is still in bed. The girl rolls over and places the pillow over her head. When she does not appear at the breakfast table her father goes to investigate.

"I have a sore throat, Dad," comes her lament.

"Let me see." She opens wide—there are large white nodules coating her tonsils. A cheek to her forehead tells him she is running a fever. He tucks her in and goes to the medicine cabinet to get some aspirin. Snuggled in her bed she feels relieved, even with her throat swollen shut. A few hours later she awakens, her throat feels slightly better. The house is quiet, her mother has not gotten up yet; it must be before noon. She goes to her closet and retrieves her paper doll collection; she makes a house of them by standing the folders on end until she has created a circle around her. Betsy is her favorite doll; she dresses her in pajamas and puts her in the fold-down bed. She is sick too. Around noon she hears her mother stir.

"What are you doing home?" are her mother's first words to her.

"I'm sick, Dad even said so."

"Okay. I'm going to get some coffee. Do you want some toast and tea?"

"Some tea would be good, but I don't think I can swallow the toast."

One of the few times her mother is kind to her is when she is sick. She is glad it is not "the bronchitis." The cough medicine they give her, Rem, is awful. It tastes like black licorice. She will hate that taste all her life.

Interlude IV

~~

THE SEATS FILL UP SLOWLY; *friends and family greet one another. Maggie watches from her bedroom; she never expected this kind of turn out; after all this is not their first dance. Brothers and sisters, nieces and nephews dot the crowd. The sun shines in an azure sky so intense it reaches into your heart and squeezes it. People shade their eyes in conversation. Pots of flowers ring the crowd. The guitarist begins: "Sunshine on my shoulder..." the bridesmaids and groomsmen file in through the arch. First, Grace and her fiancé followed by her sister, Jackie, and younger brother, Luke. As she watches her sister from behind, her mind trips over a memory. It is her mother's walk.*

7

brown

We were both skinny, scrawny kids with dark hair and blue eyes, we fought like cats and dogs, as hard as we fought we loved and protected each other, you protected my name, I fought for your honor, we were two against the world; we did not let the dysfunction of our inside life spillover into our outside world of make-believe—we ran from bad guys, rode bikes like horses out west, built forts, and fought real and imaginary enemies; from you I learned to laugh in the face of scary.

LUKE CLIMBS OUT OF HIS SICK BED. His fever has topped 103 degrees and a chill runs through him as he tosses the covers back. His younger sister stands just feet away, agitated. "Yeah, he was calling our dad bad names and then said you were a wimp and that he could take you." Luke's glazed eyes struggle to focus as he leans down to lace up his sneakers. He wobbles and his little sister reaches out to steady him. The stairs seem to weave as he starts down them. He holds tight to the railing to keep from falling. Angie, his little sister, looks up at him. "Maybe you should stay in bed till you feel better then you can give it to him." Luke just keeps moving toward the door. Outside, he walks to the curb where a small group of kids gather. One large boy steps forward and stands toe-to-toe with Luke. He is four inches taller and outweighs Luke by twenty pounds; Luke meets his gaze.

"So you called my dad a son-of-a-bitch and you think I'm a wimp?" Luke asks through clenched teeth and a red face.

"Yeah. What ya gonna do about it, ya little shit?" is the challenge from Billy the Bully. Luke swings weakly and hits Billy in the gut. Within moments Luke finds himself on the ground with eighty pounds of meanness sitting on his chest. His vision blurs as he fights to dodge blows to his head. A crowd gathers around the two combatants with cheers and jeers. A neighbor who hears the ruckus comes to investigate. He pulls Billy off of the smaller boy and tells him to go home before he calls his parents. Angie, who is crying on the sidelines, rushes over to help Luke up and take him home.

"You shouldn't have tried to fight him when you have the fever. You better stay in bed."

Luke's face is red with welts from the pummeling he took. Angie goes to get Luke some water; her older sister comes in the kitchen door as she pulls a glass down from the cupboard.

"Get down off the counter, Mom'll kill you if she sees you climbing up there. What are you doin'?" comes her older sister's query.

"I'm getting Luke some water. He's sick and Billy just beat him up."

Her older sister races upstairs to check on Luke. They are so close in age they share a connection like twins. His swollen face sets off a rage in his sibling. She runs down the stairs, letting the door slam in her wake. Half way down the block she finds Billy regaling a small troop with his bravado. Although slightly larger than Luke, his sister was still ten pounds lighter and an inch shorter than Billy but that does not stop her. The crowd steps back as Luke's sister approaches Billy with a look of cold determination on her face.

"So, I bet you feel pretty good about yourself, beatin up a little kid and all?"

Just as Billy got the "Yeah" out of his mouth her fist connects with it as she steps on his foot, causing him to lose his balance and fall to the street. She pounces on him, grabs him by the hair on his forehead and bangs his head off the ground several times.

"Still feel good about beating up my little brother, huh?"

Billy's reply is incomprehensible through his tears. She punches his face a couple of times for good measure and then gets up and walks home. Billy lies on the ground, crying, until he can find his feet and stumble home.

Up in his bedroom Luke is just waking up; one of his older sisters sits at the end of the bed.

"Hi, how are you feeling?" she asks.

"Not too bad, I guess."

"I took care of Billy for you. He won't be calling our dad any names and he sure won't be picking on you."

His sister fills him in on the details. He is a little bit embarrassed about having his sister fight his battles but he is glad Billy got his.

Luke remains in bed the rest of the night. From his room he hears his family around the dinner table, the usual cacophony of sounds rising up the staircase: plates, glasses and silverware clanging, his father yelling to watch your milk before it gets knocked over and his mother reminding them of their manners. Through the bedroom window he hears a distant voice hollering what sounds like his dad's name. It grows louder and louder until it sounds like it is right outside his room.

"John Casey!" "John Casey git out here!"

He hears the screen door slam and his father's voice rise from the street. Luke recognizes the other voice; it is Billy's father screaming a stream of obscenities at his father. All Luke can make out is something about an "amazon daughter" and "keep her off my son." Luke hears parts of his father's response, something about his daughter being half Billy's size and then something about the apple not falling far from the tree, in reference to all the swearing which is how this all got started. Luke's father has enough and goes back inside to finish his dinner. Billy's dad yells a few more expletives and retreats. Luke's siblings are warned to stay away from those particular neighbors and to play with the O'Briens whose parents are friends and who live a few blocks away. After dinner is cleared away, Luke's parents head to their nightly hangout, the bar on the corner. Mel's Bar and Grill is a long way from the Starlight Ballroom.

Luke's older sister oversees homework and teeth brushing, and then tucks her younger siblings into bed.

After that Maggie lay in her bed recounting the day. It was a release she was seeking as she bounced Billy's head off the pavement. It was not just the lack of clean clothes and fear of her parents' fights; it was a bazillion little things: not having the colored pencils to do geography map work, unsigned permission slips, no lunch on field trips, no milk money for breakfast, not enough blankets on the bed, no one home at night, the smell of stale beer, but mostly no one seemed to care. There is no place else to put this stuff pent up inside her. It comes out physically through her body. It has to go somewhere after irritating her lungs. Luke, her brother closest in age, needs the same release. Sports provide her favorite outlet; she is always organizing a football, baseball or basketball game, based on the season, and, unlike many girls, she is picked first, not last. Her natural athletic ability makes her the top choice of any team captain, when she is not the team captain, which is not often. She is the pitcher on the baseball team and quarterback or receiver on the football team. No one runs faster or hits harder. Sadly, this is a time before girls are allowed to compete so neighborhood games are all she is allowed to play.

Luke is small but plays with a lot of guts. When they can not get enough kids together for a game they periodically beat on each other, and, at the end of each fight, they smile, shake hands and laugh. Bizarre as this seems, it works for them through high school, but then comes the long struggle to find another outlet for their anger.

mahogany

Y*ou were my best friend in grade school, we were the only two families without a "ski" at the end of our names, being of Irish descent, we were treated as alcoholics-in-waiting by the nuns; in our teens, we shared talk about the Beatles, boys and shakes at the malt shop; you were my friend in spite of my bad hair and flat-chested appearance and were there for me through all of my teenage heartbreaking crushes; from you I learned loyalty and strength of character.*

Peggy turns to her best friend, "Hey, I have to check in at home before we head to your house." They are walking the six blocks home from school. It is springtime and the trees are just budding. The air is fresh and cool with a hint of the heat and humidity to come in the lingering breeze. "It'll just take a minute; I have to let my mom know where I'll be." Her friend nods in acknowledgement while adjusting her stack of books. Homework at a Catholic school is like daily penance; it consumes several hours and is painful. Idle hands are the devil's workshop, she has heard the nuns repeat often. They arrive at the O'Brien's house and Peggy hollers out, "Hi, Mom, I'm home."

Her friend is dreading this part. Mrs. O'Brien emerges from the back of the house, red-faced. "Young lady, go to your room! How many times have I told you no make-up? And what do I find in your drawer? Huh, want to tell me? What's this?" she says. Lipstick and mascara fly across the room. "Slut! Is that what you want everyone to call you? Is that what you want our neighbors to think we're raising—a slut? Is that what your father and I are working so hard for? Huh? Answer me." Her mother turns to look at her friend. "See, see, she doesn't wear this stuff, what am I? A bad parent?"

Peggy tries to get a word in but her mother has not lost steam yet.

"Wait till your father gets home; we'll see what he has to say about this. It's going to be Our Lady of Perpetual Grace all-girls high school for you next year, not some godless public high school if we can't trust you. You just go to your room, you're grounded!"

"I'm sorry, but Peggy will not be going anywhere today," her mother says to her friend. Her friend heads for the door, glad to be out of there. She feels like she is in a time warp. Each time they go to Peggy's house, Mrs. O'Brien finds an offense of monumental proportion keeping Peggy from doing anything fun. Last week, she was grounded for not making her bed, the week before it was leaving dishes in the sink. Peggy's mother had that fun-sucking puckered face. After witnessing these almost daily events in Peggy's life, she sometimes thinks her own mom is not so bad, especially when she is sober and not hung over. Her mom could be fun like the time she let her crack a real egg over her little brother's head instead of just pretending to do it. He sure was mad, but it was pretty funny.

Mrs. O'Brien leans against the door for several moments after Peggy's friend leaves. Will she pay for her sin again? Will Peggy succumb to her weakness? What will happen if she ever does the math? She must double her efforts to keep her daughter from making the same mistake she had made. Mrs. O'Brien remembers the day she declined the scholarship that would have had her strolling along the quad discussing Freud and Jung. Seven months later, Peggy was born.

Peggy is tall, black-haired and beautiful and has been visited by the boob fairy. Her friend, on the other hand, is short, mousy brown and so flat-chested she appears slightly concave. Mutt and Jeff her father calls them—she does not understand the reference. Peggy is popular with the boys, which prompts weekly admonishments regarding pure and chaste behavior from her parents. The nuns have lectured them on how it is a mortal sin to dress or act in any way that could cause arousal in a boy. Hell, at thirteen a slight breeze can cause arousal but what did nuns know. Peggy endures the onslaught of accusations and proposed retributions. How odd that her reality and her parents' appear to exist on separate planets. Other than a little make-up occasionally, Peggy avoids temptation. She does not smoke or make out with boys. She does not shoplift clothes like many of the girls her age or get into her parents' liquor cabinet. She did not understand what all the mistrust was about. Her grades are good and she sings in the choir. She knows one thing for sure: she is not a slut. She knows girls in her class who are though, they smoke, drink and make out in cars with boys and allow them to feel inside their bras. She is not one of them and does not care to be. She will tell her mother that if she ever gives her a chance. Instead all she ever hears is "Shut up and go to your room." At this rate, she thinks, she will never meet someone, marry and have children because she will be grounded for the rest of her life.

On her way home, Maggie wonders why Peggy sticks by their friendship. She is not beautiful and popular, and, at this age, a friend like that can diminish your chances of getting into the in crowd in high school. Sure they have been friends since fourth grade but she understands the politics of junior high and knows she is a liability to Peggy. Still she is very glad to have her. She hopes Peggy's mom will get over this tirade before Friday when Peggy has agreed to babysit with her for her sister Jackie's children.

9

gold

Forty chapters later I would still be writing; we have spent a lifetime saving each other; as a child you were my nurturer, protector, mentor; I grew up with your children, and your children with my child, the circle of life revisited; in the days where my mind was locked in the closet, you held me until it was safe to come out; when the closet consumed yours, I wired in a fluorescent bulb and waited; our dance is one of lead, follow and switch; we share wine and wisdom; as aging crones we mentor the emerging women in our lives; asking for forgiveness and leading with compassion; we hear each other's pains from the past and speak soothingly to them, giving them a soft cushion to lie on, opening the windows to let light in upon them, hoping the fresh air will erase their sting; we know the places that frighten us and respect each other's; we know the places that cause elation and share in them; we have seen sickness go untreated and the sadness left in its wake; you know a loss beyond all losses, where few emerge intact; strength emanates from your smile, caring from your hands; I am grounded by your stability, you are freed by my bohemian nature.

WHEN DID SHE GET THIS OLD? Jackie remembers a time, not long ago, shopping with her younger sister. She had her first real job and paycheck. Her sister needed a winter coat and no one else would see to it that she got one. They took the train downtown to Marshall Fields.

"How about some jelly slices?" she asks as they pass the candy counter. Her little sister just smiles with big eyes. This is their special treat. After paying for their selection, they wander over to the girl's section licking sugar off their fingers. They choose several coats that look warm and sturdy. They are okay, but then her sister spies one with a big fur collar. Her eyes go into overdrive.

"Can I try it on, please, please?"

She looks at the price tag, ouch. It is more than she planned to spend but the pleading eyes make her forget her budget.

"Okay, you can try it on."

It is the most beautiful coat she has ever put on, much better than those hand-me-downs from my cousins. I will look as good as my friend, Lorraine, and her mother will let me play if I have a coat like this one. The coat is a deep forest green with a fluffy fur collar the color of milk chocolate. Ten minutes later, the ten year old is struggling to step onto the escalator, the huge box blocking her vision. She misses. The big box tumbles forward with her right behind. Jackie reaches to catch her but her hand only brushes her arm. A man several steps down stops the forward progress of both the box and the child. Two big gashes run across her little sister's shins. After exiting the escalator, Jackie pulls a tissue from her purse and dabs at them while thanking the stranger for his help; her sister sniffs back the pain, takes her box from the man and walks bravely out the door, down to the waiting train, never once letting go of the box again.

WHERE HAS THE TIME GONE? Her sister is in eighth grade now and not a baby anymore and she has babies of her own ... had babies.

JACKIE STANDS TRANSFIXED, looking at the lifeless form in the small casket. Face after face floats by, lips move and then move on. This cycle repeats itself over and over until the crowd thins and then ceases. Her younger sister watches from behind the last row of seating. A new memory surfaces as each face approaches. This is barbaric, she thinks. Peggy, her best friend, hugs her. Tears stream down; the tissue she clutches is wet and wadded. Her insides feel like they have been fed through and squeezed out by the old wringer wash machine in the basement. I will never again come to one of these, she thinks. She turns to Peggy,

"This is so unfair. Why does everyone have to come stare at my dead baby nephew? Who thought of this idea? It seems so mean to make my sister go through all these hours of looking at her dead baby."

Each sentence is punctuated with blowing her nose and wiping her eyes.

JACKIE'S HUSBAND TAKES HER ARM and walks her to the kneeler. She kneels, stares, rises and follows him out to the car.

At home Jackie tucks her four-year-old in, brushes her own teeth and sits on the couch. *The Tonight Show* with Johnny Carson fills the screen. Next, reruns of *I Love Lucy* and *Father Knows Best* pour mindlessly across her synapses. "Come to bed," her husband calls softly. Her eyes are blinkless, her breath involuntary. She watches as daylight chases the darkness from her windows. A constant blare comes from the TV screen that shows only a symbol. Jackie looks down; she is clutching something; her hands open and close in rhythm.

His face is next to hers now. He leads her to the bed and she lies down and drifts into a fitful sleep.

…*Her hands lift the covers. It's here somewhere, she thinks. She searches frantically; the blanket is now a big-top tent, it has collapsed. She is under it, crawling and calling his name, MICHAEL.*

Jackie's heart races, the air is being sucked from her lungs. She screams and sits up.

Daylight streams through the bedroom window as she pulls off her sweat-soaked nightgown, pushes ringlets from her face and heads to the shower.

"It's time," he says, as he looks into her ashen face. A line of black cars weaves its way through the rain-soaked town. The headlights make wavy patterns in the reflections on the street. Thunder clouds frame the scene like a Monet cathedral against a stormy Parisian sky. It is weird to sit just feet away from her dead baby. Jackie does not want to be there but cannot express her revulsion. Words escape out the window and her facial muscles feel paralyzed. When the hearse stops she allows herself to be led to a chair under a canopy next to the hole. Jackie stares down into it, not comprehending. The crowd stands under umbrellas, a sea of black; the ocean has had its color sucked out by the billowing clouds. The priest begins "Dear heavenly Father…"

A week later Jackie stands at the stove, spatula in hand. "Where is our baby?" asks her daughter.

"He's with God," she replies, setting a grilled-cheese sandwich in front of her.

"Will we see him again?" the little voice asks.

"Yes, no, I don't know," she hears herself say. "Your lunch is getting cold, eat."

Later that afternoon, she enters Michael's nursery. One by one she folds and packs his clothing into boxes. As she folds the last blanket a piece of her drops onto it and is packed away in the attic.

TWO MONTHS LATER, Jackie's sister is sitting in her eighth-grade classroom when Sister Esmeralda enters, somber and sad. "Class, please rise, we will be saying a prayer for Paula Tomachevski and her family; her father has passed away suddenly." A stunned silence fills the room; they can not comprehend death at their age but they can comprehend the emotions of a thirteen-year-old girl experiencing loss for the first time.

For Jackie's sister it hits much closer; the still life of baby Michael in the casket continues to play nightly in her mind as she weeps into her pillow. She was his babysitter for the six short months of his life. She had cradled his head gently, ever aware of the frailty of his neck. She had fed and changed him and made funny faces to illicit a smile. Sometimes she could still feel him in her arms. Why did God let babies die? She does not pray with the class; she only moves her lips in case she is being watched. God is no longer a power to her. He has no power if he lets this happen to babies. She feels sad for Paula, but an old person dying was not the same as the loss of baby Michael.

After the prayer, Sister Esmeralda says there will be a Rosary and wake for Mr. Tomachevski at Callahan's Funeral Parlor at 7:00 P.M. that evening. The class is strongly encouraged to attend; Jackie's sister has already made up her mind: she will not be going. At thirteen she feels betrayed by her limited view of God. God is supposed to be the protector of little children. Her nephew's death is a contradiction beyond her. On top of that, bad things only happen to bad people in the Bible, but her sister is a devout Catholic and a good person, so why was her baby taken away? To Maggie this is an act of cruelty not compassion. Maybe all this God stuff is a bunch of crap.

10

sage

You saw something in me others did not; you singled me out to perform, it felt good to have attention; to so many I was invisible; this was a beginning of learning I had some self-worth; I stood bravely in front of a group and spoke, if not eloquently at least assuredly; from you I started to learn to believe in myself.

SISTER MARY CANDIDA SURVEYS THE CLASSROOM. Which one of her pre-persons could carry out an important assignment and not embarrass her in front of the whole school? Debra, a good student, sort of a brown-nose, but no spirit—too dry and lacking in emotion. Patricia? No, breasts too large, the boys will giggle through the whole thing. The greaser chicks, Joann, Katie and Jeannie, will certainly be unable to leave their mascara and cuss words at home. She mentally went row by row until row five seat two. Now there is a possibility. Skinny girl, pretty eyes, bad hair but bright and articulate, nice voice too. Actually, it will probably do her good, she thinks, to be singled out for something. Sister Candida knows she has her work cut out for her, shaping this young lady into an orator. I have chosen the perfect poem for a loner child, she thinks. This girl is different, not quite as flighty as the typical pre-pubescent. It is too bad her home life seems less than desirable, but she is serious most of the time and has a great deal of potential. Sister Candida is new to the school and has refused to read each student's file prior to the year's commencement. She likes to give them all a clean slate and not be prejudiced by others' opinions. The Mother Superior is surprised by her behavior but allows it since Sister Candida has a strong constitution and will not be as easily intimidated as the other nuns who are mostly senile and subservient.

The poem she has chosen is short but powerful. A piece from John Donne's *Meditation XVII, Devotions Upon Emergent Occasions*, entitled *No Man Is An Island/For Whom the Bell Tolls*:

> No man is an island entire of itself; every man
> is a piece of the continent, a part of the main;
> if a clod be washed away by the sea, Europe
>   is the less, as well as if a promontory were, as
>   well as any manner of thy friend or of thine
> own were; any man's death diminishes me,
> because I am involved in mankind.
> And therefore never send to know for whom
> the bell tolls; it tolls for thee.

The school talent contest is only weeks away, she will have to start practices immediately. On Monday, she takes the student aside and explains the assignment, not making it so much a choice as a dictate but Catholic youth are used to that so she takes it in stride. Sister Candida registers a note of pride being taken by the young woman, and also a bit of panic in her eyes. Well, they can work on that. They will start rehearsing right after school.

"Do you need to call your parents?" she asks.

"No, that's not necessary," the doe-eyed girl replies.

Her charge remains after school and she gives her a copy of the poem to read aloud.

"No man is an island all by itself...."

"No, no, no, you have to read what's there," Sister Candida scolds. "Now start again." The student begins again.

"Okay, now give it a little intonation."

The student launches into a singsong rhythm.

"Hold it, hold it—this isn't a nursery rhyme you're reading to your little sister. It's a wonderful treatise on isolation and mortality."

The student rolls her eyes and tries again.

Sister Candida shakes her head. "Here let me show you," she says.

"NO man is an ISLAND, ENTIRE of ITSELF!" She emphasizes the cogent terms with deep resonance. She remembers back to her debate team days and the joy of oratory. It is a lost art, she thinks.

"Remember, this is about the feelings of loneliness and isolation and about someone telling you that you matter, that everyone matters, no matter how lowly and insignificant they feel. Donne is saying that we are all important members of mankind and that our death is a loss for the entire world."

The young girl starts over and attempts to imitate Sister Candida's expression.

"Much better, much better!" Sister C exclaims.

The thirteen-year-old girl stares at the poem in her hand. She understands about feeling lonely but she does not agree that her life matters much in the big scheme of things. In fact, she is not so sure anyone would miss her at all if she was gone.

Sister C looks at her watch; they have been at it for an hour. "That's enough for today. We'll meet again tomorrow. Make sure your parents know you'll be here for about an hour each day."

"Um, sure," comes the distracted reply. There is no need to tell her parents; neither one will be home before midnight. Her little brothers and sister will be the only ones to miss her and that will be because they are hungry and want to be fed.

SHE DOES NOT SLEEP the night before the All-School Talent Show, so she practices her poem over and over in her head.

MAY CROWNINGS AND CHRISTMAS PAGEANTS have come and gone and she has never been chosen for anything; she does not want to blow this opportunity. The show is to start right after lunch.

Sister Candida gives her young protégé some final instructions about standing straight, looking at the back wall and projecting her voice. The girl peeks through the curtain to survey the audience; she hopes the perspiration flooding out of her is not visible. Her blouse is soaked to the waist. In a rare appearance, her mother sits in the fourth row. If this had been a morning event she is sure her mother would not be there. Strange, she feels no joy or apprehension at the sight. There was a time she ached to see her mother in attendance but it's too late now. She doesn't need her anymore.

The show begins with the first graders; her class will be last. She fools around backstage with her best friend, who will be singing "Ave Maria". Although she is excited about reciting the poem, she wishes she could sing like Peggy. Finally, Peggy is announced and she proceeds to center stage. Her voice is clear and rings out over the heads of the crowd. There is a round of applause when she is done. Next the young woman, hand-picked by Sister Candida, walks with head held high to the front of the stage, and, with no microphone, begins: *"No man is an island..."*

No stammers, missed lines, or garbled words; just a pouring out of a soul giving life to the words Donne wrote so long ago. The gym is quiet for a few moments following the last syllable spoken. Sister C begins clapping and the crowd follows. The young woman bows and exits the stage. Sister Candida stands smiling, inwardly congratulating herself. In that moment, poverty, humiliation and degradation fall away and Maggie feels like she can do anything.

After her successful performance, she is chosen to be editor of the school newspaper. Writing and actually being read and not ridiculed propels the young woman to put her thoughts down in a spiral notebook each evening before going to bed. Her older sister, Judy, makes fun of her, grabbing the notebook and reading out loud, but this time it does not stop her.

Peggy and she are on top of the world; graduation is just a week away. They are both excited and anxious about high school. They will be attending the public high school and that, in itself, is a huge relief. No more nuns, no more going to Mass every morning and no more uniforms, but more importantly, there will be boys and no chaperones.

Interlude V

Maggie takes her brother Sean's arm, and, holding on tight, moves first her right foot, then her left. In her brother's face she can see her father's passing, staring into the same eyes. Maggie's legs continue to support her; she squeezes her brother's hand and takes a deep breath as their shadows glide beneath the stucco arch. She looks up to see familiar faces, silent with reverence and smiling with complaisance. The sun warms her bare shoulders as the words of John Denver rub against her. She approaches the steps, carefully raises the hem of her dress and ascends. David's honestly rugged face is framed in the red rock cliffs beyond. She pauses.

"Who gives this woman in marriage?"

Maggie's brother replies, "I do." Without breaking touch she gives up her brother's hand and takes up the outreached one and moves to David's side.

sable

Y*ou were much older and I hardly knew you, yet there was a bond between us; you defended my lost innocence; you wrote me a poem, not the one I had expected, but an even better one; from you I learned some people are deeper than they let you know.*

THE MATERIAL IS SHINY SILVER WITH LITTLE BLUE DESIGNS. It is the most beautiful fabric her thirteen-year-old eyes have ever seen. There are folds and folds of it, glistening in the sunlight streaking across her bed. She remarks at its ability to travel miles from a country she has only recently become aware of and knows little about. Her brother Sean, who is in the Marines, is stationed in Okinawa. He has never been too connected to the family so he is perplexed when the request comes in the mail. His little sister is graduating from junior high school and asks him to send fabric for her dress. She has read in geography that the Orient has beautiful textiles and she wants her dress to be special.

Sean wanders the marketplace in search of just the right piece of fabric. He does not quite know eighth-grade girls tastes but he knows she has blue eyes and figures that is a good place to start. The women shove bolts of fabric at him and chatter in incomprehensible dialects. Sean nods politely and points at the ones that interest him. Wafts of the day's catch on the waterfront and the heat combine to make him dizzy as he inspects brightly colored and patterned cloth. He hates fish and its overpowering stench in the noonday sun sends him back to the barracks in defeat. He awakes the next morning, showers, and is in the marketplace by seven o'clock. It is already swarming with the sea of humanity. People haggle noisily, trinkets jingle in the breeze and bicycle horns honk to make it through the throng.

A few stalls down, a misshapen woman with few teeth chews on some kind of root and stares at him through rheumy eyes. He walks past, embarrassed by his aversion to her deformity. Her eyes do not follow but she speaks in broken English. "What you seek, I get." He stops and turns around. Still she does not look at him.

"Excuse me," he says, "I'm sorry, I didn't hear you." She repeats it. He looks at her curiously. How could she know what he wants? He doesn't even know what he wants.

She continues, "It is beautiful dress you wish to make. Is for young woman with dark blue eyes, yes?"

Spooked, he stands riveted in place. Slowly, he stutters, yyyess, yes, I am looking for cloth for a special dress."

"Come," she says, "we go back there," and she points to the darkened space at the back of the stall.

The tall sandy-haired American meekly follows the hunchbacked woman to the back of the stall where, without sight, she opens a trunk and feels her way through stacks of fabric. "Ah, yes," she says, "You like this. Here is joy you wish."

At first in the darkened booth he is not impressed. Sensing this she says, " We get light, then you see life." When the light strikes the fabric he feels a jolt; she is absolutely right—this is it. He pays her asking price, too unnerved to haggle. He watches as she pockets the money, feeling each surface, never blinking her useless eyes.

Back on the base, he carefully packs the material to be shipped stateside. A sad memory emerges and he wants to wrap his little sister in the fabric to shield her from the evil force that stole her innocence so young. He could have killed that boy and sometimes wishes he had. He shakes his head and picks up a pen. He writes a poem and places it neatly within the folds of cloth. He does not know where the poem came from; he has only written one other before and it was a silly one; this one is quite serious. It is as though the threads from the cloth are transformed into words and find their way to the blank page. Again, he stands dumbfounded at the day's events. After walking to the PX to mail the package he sits at his desk to finish some paperwork. Still distracted by his experience he chooses instead to return to the market. As he approaches the same stall he notices that someone else sits on the stool. He asks about the woman who sold him the fabric but the dark-haired man just stares, not comprehending, so he wanders into a restaurant for some lunch.

MAGGIE LOVES HOW THE DRESS MAKES HER FEEL on her graduation day. She feels important and that good things lie ahead and although her brother is a stranger to her she feels newly connected and somehow protected, again. She has many pictures taken and plans to send one to her brother to show him how her sister, Jackie, has turned the fabric into a stylish dress with bell sleeves, which are all the rage.

That feeling does not last long. With the summer over, attending a large public high school turns out to be intimidating and excruciating, but she survives her freshman year. At the end of that year comes the announcement that what is left of the Casey clan will move again. They are down to just four of them at home with several marriages and one serviceman having dropped the numbers.

The news about the move makes her furious. How can she leave her best friend Peggy? How can her parents do this to her; make her move to the country with a bunch of hicks? They probably all belong to 4-H and wear plaid flannel shirts. God, she could just die!

12

royal blue

I was the new kid in high school; you invited me to sit at your lunch table and made me a bit of a celebrity; being from the big city was exciting to you, you could not know how I was ridiculed at my first high school, what a difference; you lifted up my badly beaten spirit and bandaged my wounds.

AMY HURRIES DOWN THE HALL TOWARDS THE CAFETERIA, calling to the new girl, "Hey, are you going to join the Girl's Athletic Association?"

"Oh, I don't know, " she replies as the picture of the GAA meeting at her previous high school comes into view in her head—lots of mean aggressive faces stare back at her as she enters the room.

"Ah, come on. Everyone joins," Amy calls out.

"Well, then, sure."

"The first meeting is in the cafeteria right now. Can you come?"

"I guess so."

As they enter the cafeteria, Amy makes her way over to Kathy, Donna and Cary.

"Hey, ya joining?" Kathy asks the new girl.

"Yeah, Amy talked me into it."

The meeting comes to order. They discuss this year's line-up of sports and elect officers. Afterwards they go to Murphy's for pizza.

The new girl is elated to be accepted as part of the crowd.

"Wow, this is great. At my last high school only some ex-con-looking girls joined GAA. I love sports but could see myself impaled on a javelin if I hung with those guys. Thanks for taking me along."

"No problem, we're glad you joined. We need a good guard for our basketball team," Amy replies.

The new girl wonders if she should tell her new friends that she hopes to be a physical education teacher some day since she has given up on a career in writing; it is just too risky and she wants a secure future. Women and sports are just starting to be acceptable in 1968. God, how she loves sports; she is considered a tomboy by friends and family but she is really fitting in at this school and does not want to jeopardize her new friendships. Maybe she is just being paranoid. They all seem to enjoy sports too, and Amy is not kidding when she said everyone joins—by the attendance at the meeting she guesses that eighty to ninety percent of the school's female population was there.

How weird to be accepted. She thinks back to freshman year at Harrison High School.

"Sssh, look what she's wearing today," she hears April whisper as she enters the study hall.

"Can you believe she put those colors together?" April's friend Debbie looks over and laughs.

"Look, look, I think she's stuffed her bra today." April says loud enough for those around her to hear.

Each day is the same when she enters her third hour study hall. Usually, she ignores them, opens her book and does her homework but it gets to her.

Finally, one day she has taken all she can; as they walk out to their buses she finds herself behind April. Next thing she knows she is screaming at her, "I've had it from you. C'mon, let's go outside, I don't care if you're bigger than me, I'm sick of your snide remarks. If you want to know what size I am why don't you just ask, you pervert." Students up and down the hall turn to watch.

"Come on, Miss Perfect, put me in my place here in front of everyone—go for it."

April just keeps walking; her friend Debbie turns to taunt Maggie but this time she is not taking it. She continues to ask April to step outside if she is so tough, and if she does not like her to just say so, or maybe have Debbie say it for her. April boards the bus, never saying anything, and, thankfully, never says anything again in study hall. She wishes she had challenged her sooner instead of meekly absorbing the jibes for an entire semester.

But here she is the "new girl" being treated like some rock star. Amy and her friends want to know how life was where she came from and about the boys. She stretches the truth a bit but mostly keeps to it. Kids in rural high schools are eager for news from the outside world. They imagine it to be far more exciting than life in the country. She obliges them with stories of riots and parties, most of which she knows about secondhand, but they do not have to know that.

She remembers telling her parents that she hated them for moving, now she thinks back and realizes that out of all six moves, this is the best move they ever made.

Interlude VI

Maggie and David listen raptly as their good friend draws the crowd into the day's tapestry.

...You and I, like intersecting warp and woof, have each cast one strand upon the other's loom, and though a second pass may never be made, I thank the Weaver for this one that was. For though one's garment is not finished in his or her lifetime, mine will be immeasurably better—brighter, warmer, stronger— for the thread you gave."

Maggie gazes into the eyes that surround them, seeing the threads that shimmer in the golden reflection of the sun. She feels them weaving in and out of her soul.

13

beige

My first love; everyone has one and knows that they stick to your ribs like a bowl of chicken noodle soup; you were sweet and considerate and fun; we danced at all the dances, made out in the backseat of your car and learned a lot about relationships; you were a good first step.

M.C. M.C. IS ALL HE HAS TO GO ON. The pocket of her gym shirt has M.C. written in black magic marker. He watches her play intramural basketball; she is pretty good. She is a transfer student from another state. He is too shy to approach her. Maybe Amy or Kathy can introduce them.

It is Friday night and Randy is at a kegger in the woods. This is the perfect place for parties; the countryside goes on for miles, so as soon as the cops bust one place they move to another. Miles of country roads crisscross the county and there are far more miles than there are cops to patrol them. They have been using this spot off Highway 37 for a month.

Randy tips his can up to get the last drop and then goes in search of another beer. He is just pulling the tab when the first warning rings out, "Cops!" Everyone starts to scatter. Randy runs through the woods opposite the main road. He was thinking ahead when he hid his car on a dirt road that led to County Road H, rather than Highway 37.

He hears heavy breathing behind him and a voice. "Hey, you got a car?"

"Yeah, follow me," is his breathless reply.

He and his dad have hunted in these woods so he knows them well, even still an errant branch or two stings his face. His car comes into view in a small clearing; he hops into the driver's seat and looks up as the faceless voice climbs into the passenger seat. He is staring when she introduces herself. "Hi, I'm Randy," he manages to choke out. By the time he drops her off at her house, his tongue unties.

"Would you like to go to a movie next Friday?" he asks as she opens the car door.

"Sure, what time?"

"How about eight?"

"Okay, see you then," she says as she shuts the door.

THAT NIGHT IN BED SHE CAN'T SLEEP. She likes this guy even though she barely knows him. He's cute in a down home kind of way. The next day in school she asks around about him. All her friends tell her he plays sports, works hard and is a nice guy. She notices a slight hesitation before each friend describes Randy. When Amy pauses before responding she asks why. Amy stares for a moment, "Well, something sad happened a couple of years ago but I guess Randy will tell you when he's ready."

After their third date she blurts out—"what happened a couple of years ago?"

Randy sits stunned looking at her. Slowly he begins. "I was hunting with my brother, Jeff. I swore I had my safety on, I don't know. We were hiking up a steep hill and I slipped. Jeff was ahead of me. The gun went off. I, I couldn't stop the bleeding. I ran for help. By the time the paramedics got there it was too late."

Strangled sobs slip out.

She put her arm around him wanting to touch the sad spot in him and ease it.

When he regained composure, he continued.

"My folks were shattered but never blamed me. Sometimes I wish they would have yelled at me or something. Their forgiveness is harder to take than their hatred would have been. Jeff and I shared a bedroom. His side of the room is exactly as he left it that morning. I can't touch it. Sometimes I still think he's going to walk through the door."

IT STARTS OUT A WEEKEND THING but soon evolves into an everyday thing. Randy picks her up for school in the morning and drops her off at night after practice. She likes having a steady guy. This is her first. Being skinny with bad hair usually doesn't attract the more popular guys but Randy is different. He doesn't judge people on how good they make him look, it's simpler, he just knows if he likes you. She likes that about him. Besides, he loves to dance. Who doesn't love a man who loves to dance? But it is that sad spot in him that she longs to touch that keeps her saying yes to each date.

"Are you going to marry him?" her sister asks.

"I don't know, I suppose so."

She has been dating Randy for three years. They are seniors now. Fights are more frequent this year but she is not sure why. She is going to college in the fall; he is staying in Fall River.

Throughout high school, she has been buoyed by his status—captain of the basketball and track team, although he is not a typical jock. He is not conceited and does not like being singled out for attention; it embarrasses him. He treats her well; they went to Prom, Homecoming and most of the school dances. Randy is what people characterize as a good guy. So why can't she see a future with him? She puts down the book she has been reading for English class to ponder the dilemma.

14

laurel

> *Big ears sticking out; we called you dumbo and made references to cars with open doors; you had us read* Some Haystacks Don't Have Any Needles *and* Picnic on the Battlefield; *I wrote and you suspended the English teacher in you and applauded my efforts; from you I took permission to start sharing my voice.*

MR. K STANDS IN FRONT of his fourth hour senior English class. This is not the honors class and so his expectations are minimal. He has not tried this year's material—it is new but he knows he needs something to get this group thinking. He has struggled for years to spark students into written expression, with moderate success among the motivated, but has a bad record with those who are word-challenged. This year is going to be different. He spent the summer researching new texts and found a group that he hopes will reach those who have been ridiculed or just bored in the past. The C and D students are his focus and his mission this year.

"Your next assignment is a pictorial essay," he begins. "You can cut out pictures from magazines and books, as long as they belong to you," he adds as an aside. "You can take them with a camera or draw them, but, in the end they must tell a story. I should be able to identify an emotion or feeling just by looking at them." Hands shoot up.

"Can we use pictures from home?"

"Yes," he replies.

"How about newspapers?"

"Yes, that's fine."

"How about comic books?"

"Yeah, what about Playboy?"

"Comics are okay, Playboy, only if they're clothed," is Mr. K's response.

"Oh boo, Mr. K," exclaims a chorus of male voices.

"I didn't know they had any pictures with clothes on," chimes in one more. The clamor quiets down just as the bell rings. Well, at least they seem excited, he thinks.

Several students can be seen around campus snapping pictures; others are swiping magazines from the teacher's lounge and library. Oh well, Mr. K thinks, at least they're not leaving it to the last night. He feels something inside he has not felt in a while. He is having a hard time giving it a name. Then it hits him, he is enthused about teaching again. He is actually looking forward to his fourth hour class rather than dreading it. After twenty years of teaching, it's nice to feel that spark again.

Friday comes and the presentations begin. Chuck put up a poster board of pictures of dead soldiers and civilians, mostly women and children taken at Mi Lai. A pall falls over the class. Mr. K praises him for the powerful message his poster conveys. Several more feature Viet Nam War scenes, a reflection of the times. Some use pictures from the Kent State massacre to illustrate anger, frustration and outrage. One young woman who he saw with a camera has taken pictures of the countryside around the school, and her poster spells out "Save the Country" in pictures, and, although she uses words, the message has impact. He likes this girl; she has promise. Last year in Honor's English she had mostly slept and barely got by with a C. She has a strong A going this year and is showing a lot of ability and enthusiasm. He talks with her that day after class. She asks about books to read and he recommends

Catcher in the Rye and *Psycho Cybernetics*. She thanks him and heads off to her next class.

Later that day in the library Maggie checks out *Catcher in the Rye*. At home that night after putting Chris and Angie to bed, she reads it cover to cover and experiences camaraderie with Holden Caulfield; his awkwardness and insecurity speaks to her own. She has made a new friend. In English the next day she thanks Mr. K and shares some of her insights about the book. Mr. K finds her statements astute and encourages her to write a critique, which she can turn in for extra credit. Mr. K is taken in by her knowledge of human nature at such a young age. She tells him that although sports provide her with a physical outlet, it is reading and writing that feeds her spirit.

He wishes he could discuss books with his son but that is not to be; Adam's brain is locked away in darkness and no one seems to have the key. At least not any of the specialists they have consulted to date. Every day he looks out at the fresh young faces and longs to see Adam's among them. Instead, each Sunday, he watches him shuffle up and down the hall at St. Vincent's Home. Kids make fun of the place by calling it the Home for the Deranged or Rearranged. They have tried everything to forge a pathway through his brain to let him out: pills, cold sheet therapy, even electroshock therapy, which he and his wife almost divorced over, but nothing rearranges the chemicals or carves any paths to the outer world for Adam. Sometimes Mr. K's sadness lifts when the light goes on for one of his students. It does not happen often. This young girl with a thirst for books brings a smile to his face, but he fails to read hers.

15

ecru

Y*ou had no children of your own so you adopted us unofficially; your husband bonded with the boys, they needed it; you brought some sanity to an otherwise insane existence; you recognized my symptoms long before I did and in spite of my family's denials; from you I learned about caring for lost members of the tribe and what a home should be like.*

IRENE STRAIGHTENS THE SHIRTS AND SHORTS on the shelves in the children's department. The day is winding down and soon she can head home. Sam will be home for dinner after a day of painting houses. She scans the aisles of the store, everything seems in order. Two young clerks are cleaning out the dressing rooms in preparation for closing. One of them, a neighbor's daughter, is hanging items back on a rack.

Irene walks up behind her. "Is that the last of it?" she asks.

The girl jumps and turns around abruptly.

"Oh it's you," she says. "Yes, that's the last of the stuff from the dressing rooms." The neighbor girl pulls at the hanger to free it; it hangs up on another hanger. She yanks again and again. When she still can not free it, she shakes it violently until several shirts fall on the floor.

"Damnit!" she says as she stoops to pick them up. The hangers intertwine and fight her efforts to free them. Irene bends down to help.

"I'm fine, I can get it," the young clerk says. "I don't need your help." Irene stands up and backs away. Fifteen minutes later Irene has the bank bag ready and is turning out the lights.

A few days later Irene approaches the young clerk, this time making sure she is heard so as not to startle the girl.

"Do you have a minute?" Irene asks.

"Yeah, sure, what do you need?"

"I'm worried about you and hope you find someone to talk to soon before... Her voice trails off at the look on the girl's face.

The young clerk stares at her with a combination of fear and defiance. What would Irene know about teenage problems? She thinks to herself. She never had any kids. What gives her the right to butt into my life? I guess she and Sam have been good to my little sister and brothers. God knows, they need someone who cares.

Irene, sensing the hostility, backs off again. Maybe if she had had children of her own she would know what to do, but, well, it wasn't meant to be. After burying the third stillborn, she gave up.

Irene watches over the next week; the young girl's demeanor is increasingly agitated, and she decides to try to reach out to her one more time.

"Hey, Sam and I would love it if you could join us for dinner tonight. What do you think?"

"Ah, I don't know." A flood of emotions runs through her and something in her chest jumps. "Are you sure?"

"Yes, yes, we'd love to have you. We want to hear about your plans for college."

"Okay, what time?"

"How about six-thirty?"

"Works for me. I can check in on the kids and then come over."

The girl is suspicious of Irene's motivation, but, hell, she doesn't want to sit home and Randy is working until ten. At home she warms some leftovers for Luke, Angie, and Chris. That done, she brushes her hair and teeth and walks the two blocks to Irene and Sam's.

Sam entertains the young clerk with jokes and his clown paintings as Irene prepares spaghetti and meatballs. The spaghetti gives them all reason to laugh over dinner; no one escapes the curse of the red sauce: Irene's spot is on her chest, Sam's on his shirt sleeve and one small blob finds its way to the girl's jeans. Over dessert, Sam asks how things are going.

"Fine, I guess."

Sam stares at her and both acknowledge the lie. The discomfort forces words from her mouth.

"Well, Luke got in another fight at school. It's his second this year. They're threatening to expel him if it happens again. I tried talking to him but he just says the guy had it coming to him and brushes it off. I don't know what else to do."

Sam wanted to say this is not your problem, it's your parents, but he knows better.

"How are YOU doing?"

"Fine, I'm just fine."

Sam doesn't give up. "You seem sort of tense. Anything we can help with?"

The girl lets out a deep sigh. "I guess I'm just nervous about going off to college. What will happen to Luke, Angie and Chris, and who will look after them? She stopped herself before the next line could slip out—"who will save them from her?" Her mother's tirades spill over, attacking each child's soft underbelly. For Luke, it is his stuttering, Angie, her weight. No one escapes the barrage of insults. The only relief from the nighttime attacks is when her mother is working late at the bar or she passes out early.

Sam watches as her eyes glass over and then become cloudy. He can almost see the walls coming down.

"Oh, I'm just going to miss them. I'm sure they'll be fine. Luke is a big boy and can take care of himself. I'd better be going. It's getting late. Thank you so much—dinner was great."

"Are you sure you have to go? It's only eight o'clock."

"Yes, I have some stuff to do, but thanks again."

Outside the door she feels the tightness in her throat and chest. It feels like someone is squeezing her, making it hard to breathe. She inhales deeply, hoping to share in the night air's resolve. Her hands are shaking as she slips the key into the front door.

On Friday night Randy picks her up from work.

"Have you eaten?"

"Yeah, I had a couple of candy bars and a pop."

"That's not much of a meal."

"What are you, my parents?" she shoots back.

"Whoa, I was just asking. What do you want to do tonight?"

"I don't know. I just want to go anywhere but home."

"Okay, want to go to the arcade? We can shoot some pool."

"Sure."

They shoot a game of pool and then she asks to leave.

"Let's go for a walk. I just need to move."

They drive out to the forest preserve and walk along a familiar path. She is shivering in the eighty degree heat.

"I have a sweatshirt in the car, should I get it for you?" Randy asks.

"No, I'll be fine. What's gonna happen to my little brothers and sister when I leave?"

"They'll be fine. Luke will take care of them."

She glares at him.

"Well, what do you want me to say?"

"You know what it's like at my house. How can I leave them?"

"Hey, this is your chance to get out. You saved the money for college and you need to go."

"Who's going to do the laundry and make sure they have food? Maybe I'm being selfish. I can wait a year."

"And then what?"

"I don't know."

They walk in silence for a while. It is mostly dark when he hears her sobs and stops to put his arms around her. Her body convulses for several minutes, followed by deep gulps of air.

"I need to sit down somewhere. Let's get a cup of coffee or something."

"Yeah, where to?"

"How about Jack's Place?"

It's late July and the heat and humidity sticks to their skin like a plastic sheet. They sit in a 1950s style diner with orange vinyl booths and miniature jukeboxes. The décor is original and not an attempt at art nouveau. Their thighs meld to the vinyl booth. A couple of cups of coffee and some French fries slide off the arm of the waitress and onto their table. The young clerk is feeling weird, sort of like suffocating and tingling at the same time. After dipping a French fry in catsup she brings it to her lips; her stomach turns and she sets it down.

"What's wrong?" Randy asks.

She jumps up, a sensation of skin ripping off her thighs makes her gasp as she runs out the door. He catches up with her in the parking lot. She collapses, sobbing in his arms.

"I can't breathe" she says. "Help me, I can't breathe."

He lowers her to the ground and runs inside and asks the to waitress call for an ambulance. The paramedics arrive and lay her down on the gurney. They place a brown paper bag over her mouth and tell her to breathe slowly. Soon the tingling stops and her heart rate slows down. They instruct her to go home and rest. Randy takes her to her sister's and explains what happened. He stays with her until she falls asleep. Three days later it happens again. Her physician calls her mother back; he prescribes a heavy tranquilizer. Her mother glares as she hangs up the phone.

Back at work, Irene asks the other young clerks where her neighbor's daughter is, since she has not been at work for a few days. They say she is out sick.

"What's wrong with her?"

"Randy said she had some kind of attack or something. She says she'll be back tomorrow."

The next day Irene calls the young clerk into her office. Upon seeing the girl's grey skin and deep circles around her eyes, she wraps her arms around her. The girl initially struggles, but the pain in her wins, wrenching its way to the surface and onto Irene's shoulder. As her tears subside, Irene hands her a wad of tissue, kisses her forehead and leaves her to collect her composure.

Finally, it's the third week in August. Maggie kisses Randy good-bye, hugs her brothers and sister, loads her few belongings into her 1967 Chevy Malibu, sticks the coffee thermos on the front seat and heads to college. Before she gets out of the county her shoulders descend noticeably and her hands quit shaking.

Her first letter home will be to Irene, thanking her for caring and apologizing for refusing to be cared for.

Interlude VII

THE OFFICIATE CONTINUES...

"...*In the words of Rainier Maria Rilke, The point of marriage is not to create a quick commonality by tearing down all boundaries; on the contrary a good marriage is one in which each partner appoints the other to be the guardian of his solitude, and thus they show each other the greatest possible trust...*"

Maggie leans her shoulder into David's and holds fast to both his hands, one in front and one behind. Smiles from the faces settle her as she listens to the essence of their union: "*You don't make sense, I don't make sense, together we make sense.*" A chuckle moves through the crowd.

For so many years life did not make sense to Maggie. Its opacity and her clouded vision teamed up to keep her blinded to the small truths: there is no grand scheme, life is just what you make it each day; forcing things to happen instead of allowing them to happen only gives the illusion of control; and, finally, as noted in the Tao Te Ching, *embracing both happy and sad is freeing.*

16

burnt umber

We met the first day on campus, we were both there early, the only two in the dorm, we sat up all night talking about our Catholic upbringing and families; we had much in common; you introduced me to the inside of myself—the fear, insecurity, lack of confidence—and then said it's okay.

THE HALL OF THE GYMNASIUM is a wall-to-wall human wrecking yard. Twisted flesh of all shapes and sizes writhe like a den of rattlers. Julie finds Tad, a nine-year-old boy the size of a toddler, his useless arms and legs dangling from his father's arms. The only expression is in the boy's eyes as he recognizes Julie's familiar face, he is safe.

Julie's best friend enters the building, and, stepping around the writhing arms and legs, she locates Julie.

"I can't do this," she says as her breakfast snakes up her esophagus. "I can't, I have to go," she keeps repeating. "This is too much. I wouldn't know what to do. I can't help these kids."

Julie reaches to grab her arm as she dashes from the building, panicked and ashamed. She can not do it—repulsed and nauseated at her own lack of courage, she sits on the bench outside the gymnasium and cries.

Julie calls her friend that night and explains how the program works. "It's one-on-one. "They assign you one child to work with and you work out a short regimen for water exercise in the pool, gymnastics and motor skills, just like we do in our classes. They give you areas the child needs to work on, like coordination, strength and flexibility. You just have to put together a few exercises in each area."

"I can do that. I have lesson plans for all that stuff," her friend replies.

Julie goes on to explain, "You'll just have to modify the exercises for whatever special needs your student has and see what works. You don't get graded. Just do your best."

The next Saturday, Julie returns with her friend in tow. Her friend swallows back the panic as Julie introduces her to the program director.

"Dr. Stevens, this is my friend and she is interested in participating in the Physical Education for the Handicapped program." Dr. Steven reviews the program requirements and assigns her a girl with cerebral palsy. Her student, Sarah, is thirteen and needs to work on flexibility due to her disorder. Julie's friend works up some exercises for the pool and gym to help alleviate some of the tension in her leg muscles. During their workouts, Sarah shares her teenage hopes and fears, so, sometimes, instead of throwing balls in the gym they eat french fries in the student union and talk about boys.

"Do you think a boy will like me when they see how I walk? In junior high, all the boys tease me and imitate me when they think I don't see them."

"Well, not all boys are the same, and some of them do grow up and stop doing things like that."

"If I have children, will they have cerebral palsy?"

She thinks back to her genetics class but does not remember discussing cerebral palsy. "I can't answer that. Maybe you can ask your doctor."

"I've asked my parents, but they just say I'm too young to be thinking about that stuff."

"I don't think you're too young, but I don't have an answer. I'll ask my genetics professor about it and let you know next week if I can."

She thinks about Angie, her thirteen year-old sister, whose arms and legs function fine, but whose psyche is damaged. How would her life turn out? They finish their pops and head back to the gym to meet up with Sarah's mom.

Julie takes Tad to the pool. He likes it now but that took some doing. Tad is a quadriplegic and the size of a three-year-old. Birth defects left him without any useful limbs and a family. The latter changed; Julie is amazed that someone adopted him. Sharon and Mike have two children of their own plus Tad.

Julie gently introduces Tad's body to the water. She feels him tense and then relax in her arms. Without speech the only way to communicate is to watch his eyes and feel his body tension. The only sounds Tad can make are incoherent sort of grunting noises. While institutionalized prior to the adoption, Tad, vomited as a means of showing distress. To cure him of this nasty habit the therapist stuck Tad's head under water. Tad had come a long way in the two months Julie had worked with him. He smiles when the other kids splash him; he is beginning to hold his head up and grasp soft objects. Julie makes yarn balls for him in the evenings in her dorm room. Mike and Sharon are amazed at his progress.

After dropping Sarah off with her mom, Julie's girlfriend watches in awe from the other end of the pool as Julie moves Tad's stiff limbs in the water. She is glad she was given a girl with few limitations. She is not like Julie, although she wishes she was. Julie's disposition is so calm and level while hers is replete with rolling highs and lows. That night they share a pizza and a couple of beers. Julie's friend unloads about the scars her siblings bear.

"I hate my parents for what they did and continue to do to my younger brothers and sister. I can feed them and clothe them, but I can't fix the things that are wrong inside of them. I can handle the stuff they did to me, but it just kills me to watch them screw them up too. I feel guilty being here, but I can't stand the thought of ever going back." She pauses a moment. "Do you ever hate your parents?"

"Yeah, sure, my dad is an ass, always yelling at my brothers. They can never do anything right. He pretty much left us girls alone."

Julie grabs another piece of pizza as her friend continues.

"I hung up on my mom this week, she was so drunk. She was raging on about something I was supposed to do before I left, like fold the laundry or something. She was so out of it, I just told her to go to hell and hung up. She won't even remember in the morning. Last week when she called she told me she loved me. I think that was a first. Hey, let's get out of here and go for a bike ride."

Julie and Maggie ride down to Riverside Park, singing a John Prine song about blowing up your TV, moving to the country, raising children on peaches and finding Jesus by yourself. It is one of their favorites.

17

olive green

A rich kid with little motivation; good for a laugh and lots of beer; you taught me that I was lucky not to be from a wealthy family who gave money instead of love.

Two months into the semester Trish has not stepped foot in the U.S. history classroom. She lights up a joint and lies back on the grass. The fall air makes her reach for her sweatshirt and crinkle her nose. She hates winter—all those months indoors. She feels guilty skipping class in the winter since there really is no place else to go or anything else to do. This little park freezes up like the water on Lake Monona. She wonders where the zoo animals go when the temperatures drop to sub-zero. Surely they do not leave them out here to freeze, she thinks. Trish feels like one of the caged animals—her parent's plans for her encircle her in barbed wire. The check in the mail each month sells her soul to them. She extracts interim payments to soothe her soul or at least her psyche. A few beers and a joint or two set her right.

A friend from the dorm appears cartoonish from her vantage point—big legs, little head, as Trish peers up from the ground. Trish hands her the joint as she sits up. Her friend accepts and sits down beside her.

"I just came from the financial aid office and I'm screwed. All I can get is loans, no grants. I am so far in debt I don't think I can come back next semester."

Trish inhales, coughs and asks, "Is that a bad thing?"

Her friend sits silent for a moment. "Yeah, it's a bad thing. Without this degree my choice is to go back home to my psycho parents and get a job waiting tables or bartending in Lake Geneva. I can become a pathetic local trying to catch a rich Chicago guy, one with lots of gold chains. Yippee!"

Trish takes the last hit and stubs out the joint. "Let's eat."

"I'm broke. You buyin?"

"Yeah, sure, my folks are sending an extra check to keep me from showing up at their door."

At Mac's Lounge, her friend orders two big Macs, an order of fries and a strawberry shake.

"Shit" Trish says. "You gettin everything on the menu?"

MADISON IS THE COLLEGE OF CHOICE for all North Shore rich kids. Mad-town is known for its smoke-ins and alternative lifestyles, the best environment for rebelling against conservative, republican, parents. Her parents had tried to get her to go to Northwestern or Wellesley, her mother's alma mater, but she threw tantrums until she got her way. She planned to major in partying and there was no better place than Madison.

She pictures her mother's face all scrunched up each time they discuss her major.

"Honey, is recreation really a suitable major for a young lady?" is her mother's condemnation. "What about business or marketing? You know your father might be able to help you out after graduation in those fields."

The throbbing in Trish's temple starts up again. What an idiot her mother is. What would she know about useful majors? She majored in kissing her father's ass, Junior Service League and vodka. I should slip her a special brownie sometime. That might blow her garden party, bridge-playing mind.

Back at the dorm, they stretch out on the beds.

"Hey, I can help you get caught up in history if you want," her friend offers."

"What the hell for? It's a bunch of crapola!"

"Yeah, I know, but you need that crapola to get out of here."

"Hell, I'm shooting for the PSP, Perpetual Student Plan. I don't want to get out and my folks will keep paying, so what's the hurry?"

Her friend contemplates that last statement. All she wants to do is get done, have a degree and start a life. It both scares and exhilarates her. How in the hell is she going to get done—there is no rich Mommy and Daddy footing her bills. Maybe she can take out an ad in the local paper for a sugar daddy, someone willing to pay the bills and have a young thing on his arm for jaunts to the theatre or whatever. Shit, she is desperate and pathetic.

Trish is in a stoned slumber when she returns from her reverie. She quietly exits the room and walks down the hallway to her own room. She stops and picks up her mail, maybe Ed McMahon will be staring up at her with a big "You've Won" printed on the envelope. Instead there is something better; a letter from her little brother, Chris

> Dear Big Sis,
> I am fine. How are you? I like school. My teacher's name is Miss Carter. I like spelling and math. I miss you. When are you coming home? Thank you for the t-shirt. It is nice.
> Love,
> Chris
> PS: W.B.

She grabs a pen off her desk and some stationery, a gift from her older sister, Jackie, and begins.

> Dear Chris,
> I miss you, too. I'll be home at Thanksgiving. That's less than a month away, so I'll see you soon. Maybe you can come see me at college sometime. I'm glad you liked the t-shirt.
> Love, Maggie

She does not realize how home sick she is until she starts the letter. When she left for college she was elated. She could escape the insanity of her parents and start her own life. Those first few weeks at college were such a relief. The ton of responsibility was knocked down to only herself, not her brothers and sisters, not the mortgage, which her mother often failed to pay and she had to cover out of a minimum-wage paycheck, not her boyfriend, not her parents' nightly fights. She sleeps in peace for the first time in years. Even her roommate's snoring does not keep her up. She stopped taking the tranquilizers the doctor had prescribed for her panic attacks—of course they were not called that back then; they were called nervous breakdowns and she had her first at eighteen, unbeknownst to her.

After mailing the letter to Chris she heads over to Julie's room.

"Hey, ya got a minute?"

"Yep, just a few minaroonees, I have a study group at four."

"I was just hanging out with Trish. It sort of pisses me off that her parents pay for everything and she doesn't even go to class half the time and she's stoned most of the time. Maybe her parents should pay my tuition, at least they would get something for their money. Man, I just can't seem to catch a break."

"I gotta go. Maybe we can go for a beer later, when I get back from this group project meeting."

"Yeah, okay, see you later."

THE FINANCIAL AID SITUATION DOES NOT IMPROVE and Trish's parents are not an option. She is terrified to take out any more loans and instead drops out and gets a job. Over the next semester and throughout the summer she saves up enough money and the next fall she goes back for one more semester.

It is hard to be out of school and back in again. She lost contact with some people but makes some new friends. After a salad at the deli near campus she returns to her room and pulls out the latest story she is writing. Staring at the last paragraph she picks up her pen and continues. Her lit teacher Mr. Troy has agreed to review it when it is done.

Mr. Troy sits with mounds of bluebooks tilting to the left, about to risk the edge of the desk. He grabs them and slides them back into a reasonable stack. He can't quite get himself into the mood to grade the latest Literature 102 exams, so, instead, he reaches for the short story a young woman in his Tuesday–Thursday class has asked him to critique. She has just returned to college after taking a semester off. She wants to be a writer again, and has asked for his help. He starts in.

[Handwritten note at top of manuscript: Practice copy of story. If you get a chance check grammar. I would much appreciate it. (typing is lousy cuz I was in bad shape while doing it. please excuse.)]

The two of them sat huddled together in the bottom bunk, in a room which smelled slightly of urine ~~and mildew~~. The moon shone flourescently upon their faces, through the rain-streaked dirty ~~upper pane of the~~ window. (the lower pane was missing and cardboard had been taped in its place, rather half-assed) ~~The light that there glows figures cast haunted~~ *wes* ~~shadows suggesting a wink of familiarity.~~ *It* They sat, he craddled in her arms, in this room with bare wood floors, of coarse grain whose varnish had over a ~~century~~ *decade* ago worn off. The floors crawled up on all sides into what seemed an attempt at bl*u*e, but somehow through the too many years and too many grubby fingerprints among other things, it was rendered a dissolved grey. The walls, too, were bare and stood reflecting the others emptiness, and such ~~a vapid ugliness has never been held within four slabs of plaster before~~. It gripped at the roots of your stomach tying it in large tight knots, and left a decayed taste in your mouth. The water stained ceiling spoke of the holes above in the roof, and sitting in the middle of the largest brown-rimmed stain was an attempt at electricity, a single bulb, left exposed, dangling from a frayed cord. The meager furnishings included, the ~~before mentioned~~ bunk beds, which seemed like at any moment they might collapse, (The ~~top mattress sagged through where someone had removed some springs and left just enough to keep it afloat~~), and a dresser of drawers, its surface covered with sketchings and initials put there by some ama*a*tuer Rembrandt. ~~The drawers wouldn't be closed completely since there were no knobs left with which to grasp them with.~~

Slivers of light from the one dingy window would every now and then expose a cockroach slipping from beneath the woodwork to scamper across the naked floor boards and disappear into its sanctuary. The window faced out on the left side of the house and upon a garbage filled lot. The wind rising off the discarded piles added to the ~~disgusting fumes in the tiny box of a bedroom.~~ The air had an open highway on which to travel in, from all sides of the window frame, so wide at places that light splinters could and did ride with the wind on that highway. The cardboard didn't make much of a barrier against the bitter December gusts. The passing breezes played with the cobwebs that hung in the corner. They appeared magnificently complex, as tho each thread was geometrically placed ~~at even angles to form perfect octagons.~~ They reached down almost touching the top bunk. The wind blew in from all directions.

II

The upper bunk, covered by a thread bare blanket, ~~of a sickly pink,~~ was inhabited by Jenny an eight year old elf-queen. Her blonde stringy hair hung down about her ears and face outlining her high cheek bones ~~making them look like oversized breasts on a slender young woman, much too large to belong where they were.~~ Dark green eyes pierced your soul when you met them, but later melted into ~~a white~~ quiet pools, luminous with moonrise. Her ears protruded somewhat, through her thin layer of hair, causing her to look like an elf. She no ~~doubt~~ weighed more than fifty pounds. Her legs were rather long and gangly, tho in complete picture she was quite short. Her legs seemed to

make up three-fourths of her total height, giving her a sort of scarecrow
effect. Her thinness only highlighted the misproportions of her body.
One might think that if he was to touch Jenny too roughly, she might break.
One was also sure that if she removed her T-shirt, her ribs could easily
be counted. Her tiny frame radiated a very contradictory ruggedness as tho
toughened through age. An eight year old? It seems highly unlikely, but
eight years can be a long time if they are filled with fear and insecurity.
Remnant visions of the past still flashed in her young mind. She often
wondered if things would always be the same. Every once in a while times
would go well and inside her would settle a peaceful feeling, like the comfort
and warmth of an overstuffed mattress ladened with a patchwork quilt
that seemed to swallow you up. That's what staying at her grandmothers
was like. It was the same feeling as the smell of chocolate chip cookies
baking in Gram's oven. Life again would be fun as she sat in front of the
fireplace with her newly-bought cut out dolls.

But in the cold of the night all pleasant thoughts vanished suddenly
in a wave of cruel reality, and there she sat trying desparately to comfort
her five year old brother, Mikie. That harsh voice rang out loud & clear,
in the room. It was her fathers unmistakeable cry of wrath. It seemed
to be amplified in her elf-shaped ears. Her arms hung tightly about her
brother as she told him that everything would be alright.(Did she really
believe that)? He whimpered helplessly, not really understanding the situation,
but the abrasive inflictions shook the very depths of his empty stomach.
He wanted it to stop so he could once again escape into fantasyland. But they
only became worse. The house rattled whenever her father hurled a new
insult. The brunt of these remarks, as Jenny knew, were aimed at her mother.
Her mothers words came slow and slurred and immediately Jenny knew her
mother had been drinking...again.

In a burst of violence her father swung, striking her mother, causing her to stumble over a chair, and vile and cursed things erupted from the woman. Jenny cringed and held tighter to Mike. Could this be the same woman who just this afternoon, had comforted the little elf-queen after she had skinned her knee by falling off her bike, Jenny wondered? Mike's cries were almost audible now. Another crash was heard and more verbal garbage was slung. The elf-queen had all she could handle to keep from screaming, but she knew it wasn't her place and she feared the reaction it would bring from her parents. She wanted to run out and shake them and make them stop. These big people were her idols, they held the world together, they made everything work. Yet, the war waged on, and Jenny wondered when the inevitable belt lashing would come. During the turmoil, Jenny managed to catch a glimpse of what caused this particular uproar. The reason was a bit different from the usual one. There was something about another man that her mother had been with. The ugliness of her fathers words cut deep. Those words - "you bitch, you'll never sleep with another man again, I'll see to that," and then the belt came off. Her mother fought viciously, but the man weighed over two hundred pounds, and she was no match. Micheal was crying aloud, and frantically Jenny tried to muzzle him, as her life turned, twisted and burst hot and stabbing up into her throat. She swallowed hard, so hard that her head hurt. Miraculously, she maintained her grip and gently rocked her brother, running her hand over his forehead, and as she did, she hummed a soft lullabye, which seemed to quiet him a bit.

But the scream from the living room penetrated every board that encased
the battle. In order to keep from bolting out, Jenny lay beside Mike
and pulled the pillow over their heads. It muffled the sounds but couldn't
block them out completely.

In a moment of realization her father sat down and violent sobs wrenched
his massive frame. Her mother had run to the neighbors and called the police.
Jenny was now praying that god would make all this disappear into a bad
dream. Soon there was a knock on the door, and two large, uniformed men
entered with her mother. Her father resisted at first but then reconsidered
and left quietly. The police were used to this, outside the house they
released her father and followed him to a local motel at which they gave
him the usual warning.

Inside, her mother in a drunken stupor, entered the childrens bedroom.
Jenny wanted to hide, but where would she go? That awful stench of stale
whiskey bolted forth as her mother reached to stroke her daughters head.
The elf-queen, green eyes glinting in the moonlite, sat frozen hoping that
this woman would just leave her alone, but her mother insisted on hugging
her and speaking in her blurred tongue, words that made Jenny feel like
vomiting. Just when she thought she would surely puke, her mother stood
up and staggered out of the room. The nausea subsided and Jenny lay once
more next to her brother who had managed to escape the brutal reality
much easier than she did. After many hours of questions and confusions,
her body gave way to a distressed and fitfull sleep.

In the morning, Jenny awoke in a moist warmth, Mikie had again wet the
bed. After changing herself and Mikie, and leaving sheet uncovered to dry,
she walked uneasily into the kitchen to fix two bowls of cold cereal.
Her elf-queen eyes beheld her parent's talking quietly over a cup of hot
coffee and smiling gently at each other.

The next day he hands her his edited version. There are comments written in the margins, some she cannot read but most she can. He is reserved in his remarks as she sits across the desk from him.

"This story evokes a lot of feelings, which is good. I think you have to be careful not to overdo it. I like the line about the elf queen, it's a nice image. I think you did a good job conveying the confusion of the girl at seeing her parents all dewy-eyed after the horrendous fight. The story has merit. Get it cleaned up and I'll see what I can do as far as helping you get it published in the University Press." He stops and stares at her. "I'm sorry."

She understands his meaning; she picks up the pages off the desk.

"Thank you, I'll have a re-write for you by Friday."

It never happens, the publication that is; she is forced out again, this time by mononucleosis and money. It is years before she can finish her degree.

Interlude VIII

"...*And now to give us the true story* and the reason all of this has happened is Cathleen with the story of 'The Night They Never Met.'"

Her Story:

Maggie and I had made plans to wander the shops downtown during the Spirit of Christmas Walk an event in our town where shops stay open late, serve wine and hot cocoa and hope to cash in on the holiday sugar and alcohol buzz. After forty-five minutes of sitting at Montego's, Maggie called me. I was pooped out, my sweats and the couch had sucked me in and I was unable to move. A bit exasperated, Maggie asked whom else she could invite; she hated to waste a good hair night. Besides she had dragged herself from the couch and cleaned up. I suggested she call David an old neighbor of mine and provided his number. Maggie had met him at a couple of group gatherings and figured he would be good company. On the phone he sounded excited. The bartender asked Maggie if she wanted *another drink; figuring it would take twenty minutes or so for him to arrive, she ordered another merlot. An hour went by and he was a no-show. Defeated, Maggie headed home to the couch, dejected by having been stood up, not once, but twice in one night.*

His Story:

After hanging up the phone, David jumped in his truck and pointed it toward town. Halfway there he realized he was in his couch attire—sweatpants and sweatshirt. He turned his truck around. Now in shirt, tie and jacket he resumed his journey. Was he being presumptuous? Now the jacket and tie seemed too formal. A U-turn in the middle of Aspen Street caused some loud honking. Okay, now he has it right—sweater and jeans, not too, either way. He entered Montego's, scanned the cocktail lounge; she was not there. The bartender told him a woman had left about five minutes ago. Damn, he had missed her. He had a drink and drove back home.

Later that week, they agreed to have dinner. David apologized for being so late and the rest... Cathleen gestured to the couple standing in front of them; well, obviously, things worked out.

18

black

Cruel and just, all at once, and, later, kind; it was the times, I knew right from wrong and am ultimately responsible, just the person you wanted me to grow up to be, I am smart, you always liked that about me, not pretty, at least smart was something to brag about; you worked too hard and spent too little time with us, you stayed with her to the detriment of us; I went to college, something you wanted to do all your life; you saw me graduate gold tassels and all; I saw you shrivel recoiled in pain, lying on the couch, I gave you vitamins and whispered that you would soon be on the course again, double-bogie; your body cratered with cancerous cells that ate away your life; I lived a long time in the hole you left behind, I emerged from your strength.

IT IS 1972 AND THE WORLD IS CHANGING. Mary Ann has deteriorated and John knows it. He just does not know what to do about it. He thinks back to their meeting at the USO dance thirty-five years ago and his heart looks back at him with wet eyes. They live separate lives in the same house. There had been a few good years. John made management at the plant and they bought a new house. Mary Ann drank less and paid more attention to the children, although that was never her strong suit. She wanted a life outside the house where she could be the center of attention. That's not how things went for them. Their fortunes change with the winds of time; the country is experiencing a shift in the workforce from older management to young hotshots straight out of college and John finds himself back in the job market with limited skills. He does odd jobs and sets up a small business; it pays the bills but there is little left over. Mary Ann has taken to hiding bottles of booze in every room in the house; he knows because he finds them. At first he pours them out, but, after a while, he gives up. She just buys more and spends what little extra cash they have restocking.

It is sad to realize half his children hate him. Only a couple of them ever come to visit. Partly, it is their alcoholic mother, but he shares the blame. He was absent during their early years, working two jobs, and when he was there all he did was discipline them. Spare the rod and spoil the child, resounded in his head; he had not spared the rod; he had lost his temper egged on by his wife's ranting about how the children had misbehaved. He wishes he knew how to apologize. He is afraid to go down that road, afraid of all the blood that will need to be spilled in order to clean out the wounds. It is just too much. He does not have the strength. There are few things to look forward to; one is a visit from his fifth child who seems to have forgiven him.

John sits at the kitchen table as his daughter arrives to take to the links with him. "Is that all you have to wear?"

"Yes", she replies, eyes flashing.

He knows better than to push this topic. She is twenty and taking life on her own terms. John likes that about her, although he would like it more if she wore a little more clothing. Her white dago t-shirt and cut-off jean shorts with holes everywhere make him cringe. He ignores the lack of undergarments. What would his golfing buddies think? Oh, the hell with them. Out of eight children, she is the only athlete and the only one who will tolerate his instruction on the golf course. His other children run far and fast when he launches into one of his sermons. She alone will stay and argue with him. John likes that about her. She has changed a lot over the last few years. He thinks back to when she was younger: she was the good student and the child you could most forget somewhere. Her strange gifts of poems and pictures were out of place in a home of neckties and hankies. Moody and withdrawn and then clingy and whiny, moments later she was up a tree or building a fort. The term gay had not come to mean what it does now, but he wonders about her proclivities. Sports, Tonka Trucks and dirt hills were her favorite activities. She had dolls but they sat in the back of her closet. Paper dolls, however, were a passion; she must have had twenty folders full of them and played on cold and rainy mornings. He was glad when she showed interest in boys as something other than teammates.

By the end of the round she has his buddies in stitches. John had forgotten about her sense of humor. It really had matured since he saw her last. He has beaten her again. Although she plays softball like a pro her golf game has suffered — one good drive and then seven more shots to hit the green and put it in the cup. "Let's get a drink," he calls over his shoulder.

In the clubhouse they swap jokes.

"Why do cowboys have their names on the back of their belts?" she asks the aging doffers.

"I don't know," they echo in chorus.

"So they know who they are when they pull their heads out of their asses," she responds and the men choke on their last swallow of beer.

JOHN LIES MOTIONLESS NOW, golf clubs in the corner. It smells of life escaping. It is his breath. He mumbles and she presses her ear to his lips... nothing. She wants a sign, something to say he knows she is here but the gods of morphine hold him captive. She pats his arms, rubs his back and prays, prays for a peaceful passing, but he fights. She senses it; he is not ready to go. He is young by today's standards. They all thought he would live to be ninety so the shock is still upon them.

"Its okay, Dad, you can go," Maggie whispers. "We'll take care of each other. There's no need for any more pain. Go and be at peace. I forgive you." Several hours go by and her back aches from sitting on the folding chair at his bedside. He mumbles something again and his eyes shoot open. He gasps several times in succession, and then a loud sigh slips from his lips—it is his last. She rises, stiff, and walks to the living room where her sisters, brothers, nieces and nephews sit and talk quietly.

"He's gone," she hears herself say. The words echo in her head, sharing space with its complement heard so many years ago, "She's gone." Each of his children, in turn, goes privately to expunge guilt and forgive him.

19

silver

Each of us yearns to have this person within them, someone so totally selfless, someone that sees you, not through you, you feel present and valuable when your life is dark and scary; she never judged or flinched from your crudeness, she bore your lies and deceptions and trusted you to tell the truth, you did eventually; she served warm meals without dysfunction; you embody pieces of her because they are good, like picking items off a menu, you choose kindness and giving and looking beyond a person's flaws and finding a place for them at your table.

"Set seven more places at the table tonight. We have guests" Rosie says to her daughter Karen.

"How many are coming? Seven! Who are we having, the dwarfs for dinner? I want to sit next to Dopey."

"Hush now," her mother replies, "college friends of your brother have driven all the way from Madison."

"We only have one chicken. How are you going to feed them all? You and J. C. sharing secrets?"

"Don't talk like that," her mother admonishes. "Your brother has gone to the store."

"Dad's not going to like this; you know how he hates chaos at dinner."

"Your father is out of town on business," her mother quips as she whips the mashed potatoes.

The four girls and three guys take their places at the table and graciously thank their hostess.

"This is great, Mrs. G," echoes from chair to chair.

"Beats dehydrated camp food says a mop-haired young man. One more night of that and I was ready to dumpster dip at the campground. I was even willing to fight off the bears."

The next day as the kids go off for a hike, Rosie walks the five blocks to St. Sophia's Catholic Church and kneels in front of the Virgin Mary, asking for strength. She feels pieces of her falling off the wall like loosened tiles. "What's happening to me?" she implores. Alone again with five children, endless piles of things tugging at her—children, dishes, clothes, bills and off he goes on another trip. She prays for the thoughts to stop and let her sleep. Oh, Virgin Mary, please intercede—stop these horrible thoughts. Make me a good mother, like you. Hell, she thinks, Joseph didn't leave her for weeks with five kids and a house to run. Mary had one perfect kid who took off at thirteen. Too bad mine can't do that; I'd be down to three at home if that was the case. She immediately feels shame and guilt. She hides her tears in her handkerchief, ashamed at the kaleidoscope of failures tumbling around the end of her tube. She says a rosary losing herself to its mantra-like chant. Hail Mary full of grace...

Back at home she slides the ironing basket closer to the ironing board and begins. It's cathartic, this rhythmic motion of sliding the iron back and forth, changing things from messy to smooth. She wishes she could do the same with her life. Her older children are beginning to rebel; the world keeps inundating them with images of war and protest. It is not like when she grew up. War was honorable, and so, too, the men who served. Her husband is one of them. His plane was shot down and he survived three days behind enemy lines. She is proud of him for his dedication to his country. She does not understand this younger generation who are mistrusting of their government and question its decisions. The girls hardly wear any clothes and the boys do not cut their hair. She loves her children but feels bewildered by the loud music and disorder of things. Down deep she knows people are good and prays to God for that part of them to remain, despite political and social turmoil. Rosie likes it when her children's friends gather and discuss world events. She is impressed by their knowledge of world politics. She remembers being very naïve at their age. All the anger saddens her though. She prefers it when they bring out the cribbage board and resort to being kids. Although some days the weight of five children and a home to care for seem overwhelming, most of the time she would not change it. She loves the good-humored chatter around the table as they pass jibes during the game. Having grown up in a somber and serious home she likes the raucousness of her big clan and their friends. The young men and women from the Midwest are a good group; she especially likes the small dark-haired girl with the heavy accent.

The dark-haired girl and her son hit it off. Five years later they meet again and move in together. Rosie and she spend a lot of time talking. The girl comes from a rough background but she is sweet. She has had to drop out of college due to money problems. The girl and her son Matt eventually marry but things do not go well. Money problems plague them and Rosie and her husband make many loans which are never repaid. The girl feels terrible. She does not want to take hand-outs, she wants to work, but without a college education, jobs are low end and pay poorly. She is embarrassed and one day asks Rosie how she can repay her. Rosie says simply, "Pass it on."

TWENTY YEARS LATER, an older version of the dark-haired Midwestern girl asks a young man, "Do you know where your mother is?"

"Nope, the last time I heard anything about her she was in Arkansas, so maybe she's still there." The young man scratches the new stubble on his sixteen-year-old chin.

"What about the family you're staying with, can you go back there?"

"Naw, they hate me. All the dad does is yell at me and I feel like I'm a hassle. They already have three other kids; they don't need me. I think they're just doin the minister a favor by takin me in."

"Well, I have a spare room and if you stay in school and get a job you're welcome to it. I'll help as best I can, but you have to promise to stay out of trouble: no drinking, no drugs."

"That's fine. I don't like that stuff anyhow."

"Go get your bag; I'll get the room ready for you."

Wearing baggy pants, Eminem hat and South Park t-shirt he throws his bag on the bed. Maggie tries not to judge; they all look like that these days. He leaves with a buddy, spitting gravel as they careen down the driveway, engine gunning. She cringes. She has not raised any boys, except maybe her brothers, but that was a long time ago. This will be a challenge. Inhaling deeply, she remembers the words spoken by a lost young woman borrowing enough money to cover the bills, one more time, "How can I ever re-pay you?"

"Pass it on" was the reply.

She is passing it on.

Interlude IX

"... Listen as our spirits and the canyons are filled with 'Annie's Song.'"

> *You fill up my senses*
> *Like a night in a forest*
> *Like the mountains in springtime*
> *Like a walk in the rain*
> *Like a storm in the desert*
> *Like a sleepy blue ocean*
> *You fill up my senses*
> *Come fill me again*
>
> *Come let me love you*
> *Let me give my life to you*
> *Let me drown in your laughter*
> *Let me die in your arms*
> *Let me lay down beside you*
> *Let me always be with you*
> *Come let me love you*
> *Come love me again...*

It was John Denver and the lure of the Rocky Mountains that drew Maggie to Colorado all those years ago.

20

fire engine red

Big and blousy comes to mind; you lived life on your own terms, or at least that was your rationale; you were an island with no port, loud and cocky, you pushed your way through life, leaving broken hearts strewn along your path; the fortress around your heart withstood the barrage and you remained a being beholding only to yourself; from you I learned how to keep the coffee hot and take down the walls or be ready to inhabit my planet alone.

PHYLLIS TAKES THE NEW GIRL UNDER HER BEEFY ARM. My God, she's green, some sweet thing from the hills of Iowa or somewhere like that, she thinks.

"Grab a tray of cups and some of that rolled up silverware and follow me, sweetie." The new girl stumbles over the floor mat and almost spends her first paycheck on cups. Phyllis launches into her gospel: "Honey, put four cups on each booth and table. Keep the coffee maker going and don't let a cup go dry. Watch out for Happy Hands Harry, grabbin' a cheek keeps him smiling all day. Make sure Neal at the front desk gets his lunch on time and find a decent pair of shoes or your dogs'll bark all night. You'll work seven to three Monday through Friday. You'll set up for lunch and dinner. If you want any extra shifts check with Paul, he'll be gone after each new snowfall, so you can cover the three to eleven for him. Any questions?"

The new girl blinks and takes a deep breath as she surveys the coffee shop. She has waited tables before but not at a coffee shop. This should be interesting. The orange vinyl booths, miniature jukeboxes, avocado green walls, and the fifties-style counter make her chuckle. Cups sit upside down on trays and the ashtrays are stacked on the shelf above them. The smell of grease permeates every surface and she feels it crawling under her skin. She is already mentally writing in her journal. Phyllis will make a great character in her book and v-neck Paul, with his scrubby blond hair sticking out of his t-shirt, is sure to be worth a few lines.

"No, no I think I have it. Thanks."

PHYLLIS TUGS AT THE CAP of the container. She just needs one to get through her shift, she tells herself. The nightmares have returned. How long had it been? She knows the answer only too well. Noah would be sixteen tomorrow. The tears back up in the corner of her eyes and refuse to move, like the pain in her chest that squeezes until she holds her breath to still its grip. She holds tight to her thoughts and wills herself back to the dining room.

Her apartment is dark when she enters; she reaches for the lightswitch instinctively. Something soft brushes against her leg and she reaches down to pick up Scraggly, her thirteen-year-old tabby. She tosses her mail on the table, sets down the cat and heads to the kitchen. The dishes from last night are stacked on the counter. She reaches for a clean glass, none. She runs a dirty glass under the faucet and refills it with bourbon and ice. In front of the TV she flips through the channels while plopping down on the couch—nothing, as usual. The first gulp burns her throat in a good way; it is purging the day from her mouth, ridding her of the taste of chicken-fried steak and burgers. She realizes she is greasy. It gets into her pores even though she only serves it. The bottom of the glass meets her gaze and she rises to replenish it. The kinks in her neck are loosening, the warmth of the bourbon acts like a good masseuse. She avoids the picture staring at her from the living room wall. The eyes feel like they follow her. A big slug and she digs into the dishes, rinsing, stacking and wiping. Her bra is digging into her ample flesh so she heads to the bedroom and off it comes, along with the jeans. She slips on sweat pants and a t-shirt thinking that this should be the universal uniform.

Back on the couch she surveys the selection on TV, hoping to find something inoffensive and mind-numbing to serve with the bourbon. She is on her third when she hears a noise in the hallway, Scraggly comes running after a loud thud sounds. Damn cat, knocked down that candle again. She dozes off.

The phone rings, "Hi Mom, what ya doin? Have you gotten my presents yet? What kind of cake are ya makin?"

She struggles to answer but in a panic realizes she has not shopped yet or bought the cake mix. No, she makes carrot cake from scratch; it is his favorite. Phyllis's head jolts upright and her eyes pop open. She is shaking as she walks to the kitchen to pour another. Let's see carrots, brown sugar, butter, cream cheese. She pulls bowls from the cabinet, cake pans from the oven drawer. The flour bag tears as she opens it; the counter is covered with the fine white dust. Furiously, she grates, adds and mixes. She pours the lumpy mixture into the rectangular pan and puts it in the oven.

"Its okay, Noah, baby, your cake is in the oven," she slurs.

She looks at her glass—empty. Didn't I just fill it? She wonders. Must have forgotten. The bourbon bottle is low; she pours the last into the iceless glass and stumbles to the couch. A loud screeching sound and coughing wakes her. Scraggly is on her chest, licking her face. Her eyes burn as she tries to focus them. Smoke, why is there so much smoke? She staggers to the kitchen following the trail of haze. Why is the oven on? She opens the door to plumes of black fog, grabs the pan. "Ouch, damnit!" She grabs a towel, pulls the pan out and takes it to a window. The shriek of the smoke alarm is piercing her brain. She waves a towel under it and opens all the windows. There is a breeze tonight so the room clears as she surveys the mess.

"He's gone, he's gone, I killed him," she cries as her back slides down the wall until she is sobbing on the kitchen floor. She feels her muscles tearing from bone as her chest heaves; she vomits and lays her head back against the cool plaster. Her head hurts and her back aches. She crawls to her bed and collapses.

In the morning she calls in sick and goes back to bed. Around two o'clock in the afternoon, she feels for the faucet and steps into a hot shower, a litany of guilt running like credits in her head. She has to stop drinking or at least cut back. In a towel she walks barefoot to the kitchen. The mess turns her stomach, but she swallows hard and does her penance.

THE YOUNG WAITRESS HUSTLES PLATTERS of bacon and eggs, coffee and toast, back and forth to the service window. Blond and tan, Paul proffers wisdom from the other side of the opening.

"She calls in every year on this day. We expect it."

"So why didn't you schedule more help if you knew she wouldn't be here?" she shot back.

"Just wanted to see you run your ass off, new girl, see what you're made of," comes his sarcastic retort.

"Hey, why does she call in on this day each year?"

"Today would have been her son's birthday." Paul replies. He died in a car accident — Phyllis was driving."

"Oh," is all she can think to say. She picks up the tray of cups and begins resetting the cleared tables.

The next day at work, Phyllis looks like death on a bad day. No one says much and the new girl keeps busy and stays out of her way. She is surprised when, at the end of her shift, Phyllis asks if she wants to go get a drink.

"Um, sure, where would you like to go?"

Phyllis thinks for a moment. "How about the Kick and Stomp over on Bannock?"

"Sounds good to me. Give me a couple of minutes to clean up and I'll meet ya there."

Kick's is a typical cowboy bar: saddles and stuff on the walls, jukebox in the corner, pool and foosball tables and a dance floor. Phyllis buys the first round and launches into a tirade about the owners of the coffee shop. "They're so cheap, their pennies ask for change." The young waitress just nods since she has yet to meet the owners but suspects Phyllis is right, based on her wages. A few drinks into the night, the young woman approaches the subject of Joe. She is curious about this man who is clearly smitten with the big redhead.

"Why don't you take Joe up on his offer? He seems like a nice guy."

A brief light flashes in Phyllis's eyes, but her answer comes softly. "Aw, he just ain't my type."

"So, what is your type?"

"I like my men a bit rougher, not quite so sweet. I don't want a man who is just so darn nice all the time."

"But don't you hate being alone?"

"Oh, honey, I'm not alone..." Phyllis stared into her beer a moment. "Well, anyway, I like my life the way it is. So why don't you have someone? You're a sweet young thing."

Maggie considers the question while she contemplates the bubbles in her beer.

"I've met someone but I'm not sure where it will go, so I'm keeping my options open. He's a musician and you know how that can be."

"Yeah, that's the love 'em and leave 'em crowd. I've dated a few of them."

"Besides, I'm like you; I like my life free of encumbrances. I learned a long time ago to take care of myself, so I don't need someone messing things up."

The band returns from break and the two women pick out a couple of cute cowboys and hit the dance floor.

21

chameleon

Master of the half-truth and terminal victim of yourself; I fell in love with the music and married the man, oh how life repeats itself; I hated myself for you; you took my disease and gave it a medium to grow in, we were everything I never wanted to be; my self-loathing gave way to self-realization when I grew out of you, your sickness enabled mine until my prayers to the great spirit were answered; the answer was simple: do the right thing, I did and healed, although it took years; from you I learned to throw off my crutches and walk my own path.

MATTHEW HITS A SERIES OF NOTES on his electric keyboard in his boyhood bedroom, the one with the baseball players on the wallpaper and sports trophies on the shelf. He hears his father outside mowing the grass. One more thing he'll get chewed out for; he was supposed to mow it yesterday but forgot.

Matt is unemployed again and thinks maybe he'll try music; again. He and his buddy John have a gig at a local hangout tonight. It doesn't pay much but it's some exposure. It's better than the damn warehouse job he just lost. The boss was a jerk. He was only a couple of hours late and he had a good reason—his truck broke down. What was he supposed to do? The damn alternator gave out. His dad's mechanic told him it was going a few months ago but he did not have the dough to fix it. His paycheck never goes very far. Some new sheet music and a couple of beers do it in. The guy had it in for him anyway. Matt thinks about a friend who owns a ski shop in a small mountain town if enough gigs don't come along. He could probably work in the rental and repair shop. He is a maniac on skis and lives for the snow.

At twenty-five, he sure wants a place of his own. His parents are just so fifties. His father is always ragging on him about his hair and friends. He's not going to cut his hair just because the old man says so anymore. He's sick of his uptight, conservative bullshit. This is the seventies and the world is changing. Matthew protests the war in Viet Nam, which infuriates his father who fought in WWII. He is not a coward, just because he doesn't want to go kill innocent women and children. He definitely has to get out of here.

He had a place right out of high school having married his first girlfriend. It only lasted six months before they both realized it was a mistake. After that, a short stint in college had him hating dorm life and architecture, his intended major. He moved back home figuring on getting a job and his own place. That was two years ago.

The middle-class neighborhood he grew up in is full of well-manicured lawns, matching lawn chairs, backyard barbecues and swing sets. Front porches hold brightly blooming flowerpots and swings. Neighbors are friendly, but not too friendly. Everything has the appearance of order and control, but Matthew knows what goes on behind some of those doors. He grew up with the children who wear the scars of abusive fathers and alcoholic mothers.

What did their fifties brand of ideas get them? Matt runs the litany of all the things he hates about his parents' life through his head: shitty dead-end kiss-the-bosses-ass jobs, excessive mortgages, ulcers, headaches, status cars, kids they don't know or understand, bullshit love it or leave it American beliefs, blind faith in corrupt leaders, a god who sucked all the fun out of life and empty marriages filled with boredom and disappointment.

Matthew wants something else, something different, he thinks. He does not want to live a life of quiet desperation.

He heads out for a walk when he hears his father slam the back door and lights up a joint out in the park down the block. Maybe he'll go on the road and check out some new places. He can hock a few of his father's tools and buy a VW microbus. He'll never miss them, hell, he never uses them. He's sick of hearing about getting a steady job and settling down. His old man thinks his way is the only way. He's not going to be judged by his father's standards. They are not his; they are the yardstick of cranky old men who have had the life siphoned from them.

How long has it been, he thinks, five, maybe six years since then? The VW bus only made it to Salt Lake before blowing up on the interstate. His father had to come bail him out again. The music didn't pan out either, just not enough steady work and the pay was worse. Besides, now he is married and has a kid. He had stopped in at a coffee shop one day and met this cute waitress. Turned out she was one of the group from the Midwest who had come out to Colorado on spring break with his best friend Jeremy and had dinner with his family. They dated for awhile and then decided to get married. A year later a baby girl came into the world.

He is getting a lot of heat to find a steady job, now that he is a father and all. His friend Jim invites him to Crested Butte, Colorado to work in his ski shop, so they pack their meager belongings in their 1960 Dodge pick-up and head west.

He and Jim put away their tools and head uptown for a beer. Quitting time in a ski town is the best—everyone meets at the Crusty Butte Saloon for a few cold ones.

"Hey Eric," Jim calls out as they enter the dark and cool. "Two MGD's and a basket of nachos."

"You got it." Eric barks back.

Jim turns to Matt. "Sure hope that damn truck gets here with the new inventory for this season by tomorrow or you'll have to take a few days off till I can keep you busy again."

"Crap, I can't afford the down time. The little woman will be all over me about the money," Matt says in response. "Shit, a few days off work and it takes a month to catch up."

Jim nods in sympathy. They toss down a couple more beers and head for the door. They drive two blocks to the Canyon Liquor Store and pick up a couple of twelve-packs. Jim jumps back into the driver's seat, talking as he does. "Can't figure out how two more pairs of skis disappeared. You locked up last night, didn't you?"

"Yeah, I locked up tight—doors, windows, everything. Are you sure they didn't get sold?" Matt asks Jim.

"I went through all the receipts and I don't have one for either of them. I saw them last Tuesday when I did inventory and now they're gone. It just doesn't make any sense."

Jim guns the truck up his driveway. Matt's wife and daughter sit in the old Dodge pick-up. "I hope she's not pissed, we were supposed to be here at six o'clock." Matt looks at his watch; it's 6:45 P.M. She'll live.

Jim and Matt and his wife cut veggies, start the grill, marinate the meat and set the picnic table. His daughter chases the dog around the yard. Jim's dog runs circles around her and barks.

They heap plates with elk burgers, salad and beans. Matt volunteers to get another round of beers from the fridge.

"Everyone dig in!" Matt calls over his shoulder.

As the sun disappears behind Elk Mountain, Maggie rounds up their daughter and packs up the car. Jim is still puzzling over the recent rash of disappearing skis and boots. Matt just shrugs his shoulders and looks away.

The next day Matt heads off to work while his wife gets their daughter ready for summer art camp. She will have a whole week of uninterrupted cleaning and organizing. She is going to start in the garage so she can make room to get things out of the house. She puts together some metal shelving and begins stacking assorted paints and solvents. Next is a pegboard for tools. Soon the floor appears. She hasn't seen it since they moved in four years ago. The ring and outline of an opening surprises her. She does not remember extra storage under the garage. She tugs on the ring—stuck. She bangs the edge with a hammer. The ground moisture must have made it swell. She gives a mighty yank and almost falls on her butt as it gives way. The darkness below allows only shadows to be visible. She grabs a flashlight. Maybe I'll find buried treasure, like that vault they found in Chicago, she thinks. She has forgotten it was empty when they finally got it open.

As the light bounces around the darkness, she catches a glimpse of shiny objects. The crawl space is only a few feet deep so she hops down after checking for unwanted vermin. She stoops down and swings the flashlight back and forth. A strange numbness drops her to her knees as her mind struggles to take in the view. He didn't, she thinks, but the evidence slaps her in the face: row after row of skis, poles, boots, all the things Jim has described as missing. But Matt and Jim are best friends, have been for ten years, this just doesn't make any sense. Suddenly, her brain unfreezes and an avalanche of thoughts bombards her: disappearing jewelry, lost paychecks, missing money—she sits back, using her hands to steady her.

She goes back into the house, sits on the couch and puts her head in her hands. Has he been lying all these years? How has she missed the signs? How is she going to confront him? Maybe she should just take her daughter and leave. She is sick of living in poverty, borrowing money and never being able to pay it back. She is in between house-cleaning jobs. She could go back to her family; her sister would help her out. But then she will have to admit failure. The last thing she wants to do is to admit she was wrong about her choice of lifestyle. She left her Midwestern family to seek new adventures and to break out of the mold. She never wanted to live like her parents. Her life would be different, defined as better. Maybe Matt can get help. Damn, she does not want to raise her daughter alone and she has vowed not to be a divorce statistic like so many others nowadays. Besides too many people of her generation are taking the easy way out and splitting up. She wants her daughter to grow up in a two-parent household, not a product of one of today's blended families. His parents are another consideration. She loves them; they are the normal parents she longed for; how can she leave them? Tears of confusion spill through her fingers. She thinks back over the years with Matt. He is not a bad guy, lazy, but never abusive, at least not physically.

What the hell am I going to do?

Over the course of the afternoon her anger flourishes. That night Matt is welcomed with the silent treatment. The words are all packed together in her throat, no one word taking the lead; they just sit there, preventing her from speaking. Matt makes a few attempts during dinner to free the logjam in her throat. Finally, defeated, he storms out of the house and down to the bar for a drink. Fine, she thinks, isn't that just like you? Just walk out—that will solve the problem. She continues to stew until Matt walks in at two o'clock in the morning and then the jam breaks.

"How the hell could you?"

"Could I what?"

"Don't act like you don't know what I'm talking about? You stole from your best friend! Your best friend!"

"What the hell are you talking about?"

Red-faced from his denial, she picks up a book off a nearby shelf and throws it at him. Matt ducks and the book lands with a thud on the floor.

"What, do you think I'm stupid? I found them, all the ski equipment Jim said is missing. They're under the garage. You're a thief!"

Matt's mind is racing.

"Wait a minute. Some of that equipment is mine and the rest I'm just storing for Jim. You can ask him."

"Bullshit! I heard him say they were missing just the other night."

"No, no, he found those. Jerry, our stock boy, had just put them in the back room without telling him. You can ask him."

"I will, so you better not be lying. Where did you get the money for the equipment you have? We can't even pay the rent."

"I traded work for them. Remember Jack? He made me a deal for them."

She can not remember a Jack but the night is wearing on her. Her rage begins to dissipate with her energy.

"Where did my mother's wedding ring go?"

"What the hell are you talking about?"

"It's missing. Where did it go?"

"How the hell should I know? I don't even know where you keep that stuff."

"Well, I'm going to ask Jim tomorrow about the skis and stuff."

"You do that."

She is suddenly very tired. "I'm going to bed. You can sleep on the couch until I check this out."

"Go to hell, I'll sleep where I want. This is my house too, you know."

Matt is six and a half feet tall with blond hair and big biceps. Although he has never been physically violent, she is intimidated just the same.

"Fine, then I'll sleep on the couch." She grabs a pillow and blanket out of the closet and stretches out on the couch. She hears Matt slam the door several minutes later. She is too tired to give a shit where he goes.

In the morning, she wakes, startled and aching. Her daughter is standing next to her asking for breakfast. She stumbles to the kitchen and makes some oatmeal for her daughter and some coffee for herself. Her hands shake as she raises her cup to her lips. Halfway through the first cup she jolts upright in her seat. She runs out to the garage and pulls open the trap door. Damn, why hadn't she counted the stuff yesterday? She is sure some skis and a red pair of boots are missing. Back in the house she ponders her dilemma. How can she tell Jim? What if it is true? Matt will lose his job and then where will they be? They are already in serious financial straits.

She wrestles with her conscience all day and decides to let it be unless Jim says anything else. Maybe Matt returned the stuff and then it would be alright. Going forward, she will keep a close watch on him and their things.

When Matt comes home that night nothing is said. They each consume a couple of beers and watch TV.

Interlude X

"...Now the groom's sister, Pirie, will read the list written by Maggie describing what David brings to this relationship."

- Dave droppings—little sayings out of left field that hit the mark
- Life outside the box—someone once said David lives outside the box and visits once in awhile
- Ironing at the other end of the board and one pile fits all laundry
- Lip attacks (means he needs a kiss)
- A wonder at each day's rising
- Gentleness, courage and strength
- Hard work and willingness to partner
- Love of family and friends
- Sweet love letters delivered at dawn or stuffed in my suitcase
- Flowers and Eiffel Towers
- Patience and calm in the storm
- The artist's eye
- The words of a poet
- The heart of a romantic and
- Unconditional love

22

evergreen

You wrote to me during my darkest days and told me I was a champion in your eyes—how could that be; you sent me fifty dollars for retail therapy knowing that for women this was akin to a dose of Prozac, showing me the depth and dearth of your knowledge of the subject; it was perfect, I always respected you but when you became human, I adored you.

RICHARD STANDS IN HIS WORKSHOP, tool in hand, and looks around. Now where did he set the sand paper, he wonders. He feels anger rise and grip his chest. Fear follows in its footsteps. He picks up several boards while searching, turns around several times and tries to trick his mind into remembering. He feels the all too familiar flutter that momentarily takes his breath. Did he take his pills this morning? Again, no response. Finally he gives up and goes to the drawer to get a new piece of sand paper. The toy train sits assembled on the workbench. He takes each piece in turn and applies the fine grit paper, the last step before he applies the stain. His grandson will be the happy recipient on Christmas.

There is a soft knock on the door. It is a young woman. Oh, yes, it is my oldest son's first wife (if you don't count that right out of high school thing, which he doesn't), he thinks. What is her name again? Oh yeah, Maggie, he answers himself. Sad about the end of the marriage, but they remain family, bonded by brown curly hair and blue eyes—his granddaughter.

"How is Grace's dresser coming along, Dad?"

"Oh, it's drying over there. He points to the far corner of the shop. "I've finished the frame. Just have to get the drawers going now."

"Wow, it's beautiful. She's going to love it. What are you working on now?"

A moment passes, so she asks again, knowing his hearing is failing. This time it registers and he points to the train on the workbench.

"Who's that for?"

"I'm making it for Jesse. After I made one for Jonah for his birthday, Jesse had a fit, so I thought I'd better make him one."

Richard thinks back many years, to a time when he first met his daughter-in-law. She had dropped out of college and moved to Colorado. His son brought her over one evening after they met at a coffee shop. They owned an older home and were stripping wallpaper in the dining room. She offered to help, so, side by side, they sprayed water and scraped. He recounted his World War II stories for her. His plane had been shot down behind enemy lines and he spent three days hiking to safety. They drank iced tea and had a contest to see who could get the longest continuous strip of old paper off. She appeared to genuinely like his stories so he told more: how his brother and he had stowed away on a ship out of Ireland to come to America and how he and his wife had met.

His daughter-in-law watches as he gently sands the toy train. She remembers his stories from so many years ago. She loves them all and asked him to repeat them for her daughter. Her family history was not the kind you asked to repeat or shared with your daughter, at least not until she was older.

That was almost twenty years ago when his memory was just starting to show signs of deterioration. She thinks back to her nervous breakdown, the big one. His support and unconditional love both surprised and astounded her. Here she was, half crazy, and he was telling her how proud he was of her because she had identified a problem and sought the help she needed to overcome it. With an arm around her shoulder, he reassured her that she would be fine. His strength reached out to hold her as she learned to walk on her own for the second time. The day she was released from the hospital, she made up her mind to take back control of her life, or maybe establish control for the first time, she was not sure. It was not easy and some days she narrowly avoided head-on collisions with the past, but she and her daughter were doing fine now and the dark no longer frightened her.

Now she worries about her ex-father-in-law. How can she return the favor? She sees his fears: losing his eyesight and memory; no longer a valued employee; unable to hike and fish. All the things he used to define himself as a man are disappearing. Some days when she visits he doesn't know who she is and it saddens her. She wants to put her arm around his shoulders and tell him everything will be alright, but he is a realist and she does not want to insult him. Instead she walks over and puts her arm around his shoulder, kisses his cheek and says "I love you."

23

azure

Do da dee da (translation: good idea), you kept crayons and coloring books for my daughter, my only friend to acknowledge her; you drank yourself to death—why; you drew beautiful houses and wildlife alone in your room; I keep crayons handy; you never know who might come through the door of your life; be ready to color.

MARTY AND KIM SIT AROUND THE KITCHEN TABLE, quiet. Marty breaks through the silence first. "I'm going to be drafted so I might as well sign up so I have some kind of choice of where I end up. I don't want to go to Nam. I know it's going to interrupt my schooling and wreck my chances of getting into law school, but at least I'll be alive."

Kim feels a numbness crawl up her brain. This is not part of the plan. He is going to be a lawyer and she will teach and raise a family. She had not thought much about the war, but now she hates it, not because it is wrong but because it wrinkles the sheets of her neatly made bed.

"Can't you wait and see? It's only two years if you're drafted."

Marty feels the red creep up his neck. I could die in Nam and she's worried about life in suburbia, he thinks. His stomach flips over and he swallows hard to keep it down. Marty glares at Kim. "I'm enlisting tomorrow."

Marty orders another Budweiser and slides a ten dollar bill across the bar. He has not thought much about the years before the army. It is as though it is someone else's memory he has intruded upon. Being a lawyer in suburbia with two point three children and a trophy wife makes him want to laugh and vomit at the same time. Laugh because of his naiveté and puke at the smugness of it all.

The small art gallery he opened is doing well and he is even selling some pieces for big bucks to the tourists. His move to Crested Butte in '73 was worth it. He heard Kim went on to marry a doctor. How perfect!

Marty gathers up his change, tosses a dollar on the bar and heads home; a few minutes after getting home, a friend and her daughter stop by to talk. The little girl runs into Marty's outstretched arms; he picks her up and twirls her in the air. "Ready to color?" he asks.

"Do da dee da" is the reply from the curly-headed two-year old. "Jouche, jouche," she cries.

"Just a minute, I'll get you some." Marty comes back into the room with a glass of orange juice and hands it to her. After a few fast gulps they set upon the Winnie the Pooh coloring book with crayons in hand. As they color, his friend heads to the kitchen to get coffee. Maggie refills his cup and retrieves a clean one for herself. A faint whiff of alcohol barely registers as the fresh coffee hits his cup.

After they leave, Marty adds a dash of brandy to his coffee and picks up his pencil. On his drawing board is the beginning of an eagle, a lightly sketched outline. He takes a deep breath and begins to fill in the detail. Fifteen minutes later his legs start to tingle so he shifts positions. The eyes and mask appear with a few more strokes of the pencil. Marty gets up for a refill, stubs his toe on the stool but does not notice. Back at his desk the haunting eyes stare up at him. He stares back and through. In his next life he wants to come back as an eagle, with eyes that can spot a dime at six hundred feet and wings that allow him to play on the wind, alternately floating on thermals and diving to the ground for a quick meal, and rising again and again, darting earthward in a death dive only to pull up at the last moment before impact, reflexes driven by instinct instead of deadened nerves. He shakes his leg again to get sensation.

The pencil makes little waves depicting feathers; he darkens the edges and draws talons to hold it to the barren tree branch. His mind pushes away thoughts of last night. It did not work again, no matter what she did. Maybe she would just quit calling or maybe he would just not answer. He likes the smell of her, clean and safe, her skin lightly tanned with freckles in funny places, like on her knees, lower back and one big one below her navel where it meets the blond fluff. The softness in his pants sits like incriminating evidence of his growing dysfunction.

Marty puts his pencil down and finishes his drink. He stares out his bedroom window, trying desperately to see his life, his future, anything. Giving up, he slides his increasingly useless legs from under his desk and crawls into bed.

At forty-nine, his family buries him. The damage to his nerves caused by a skiing accident and too much alcohol never heals. His legs become increasingly weak and sex is no longer possible, so all that is left to do is drink. Soon Marty and the pain, physical and emotional cease.

His friend and her daughter, now thirteen, were miles away when they got the news. The loss, the waste, the memories sadden both. They wonder what made him choose death over life or maybe disease over health; either way they will miss him. They pull out a coloring book and crayons in his honor.

Interlude XI

"*...and now the list written by David of what Maggie brings to this union. It is read by Maggie's sister Jackie.*"

- *The wonders and discovery of being part of a family... Sweet Grace and her fiancé*
- *Wisdom—learned from hard-fought life experiences*
- *Common sense learned from life and the teachings of the Tao*
- *Her patience to let others become what they will be and do what they will do*
- *Encouraging me to believe that "life holds no age limits"*
- *Her insatiable passion for living every moment of life*
- *Taking me kicking and screaming to the gym*
- *Her creativity and her amazing gift of writing*
- *Her ability to love and respect unconditionally*
- *Her generosity and need to pass it on*
- *Her turned-up smile that still melts my socks*

- *Sitting on the living room floor reading to each other*
- *Saying "Yes" to my lengthy proposal*
- *Her sense of humor and finally*
- *Her beautiful sweet self*

24

marigold

The best comedian in the mountains; had you pissing your pants with one liners; partners in crime till life took us in different directions, we share moments now but we are much more subdued; once in awhile we are young and crazy again, swapping one liners; like cream, you keep my dark serious side more a latte than an espresso.

CATHLEEN WATERS EACH PLANT ON THE FRONT SHELF and gives each one a pep talk. She believes in talking to plants, not because it helps them but because it helps her. Her days at the Flower Pot can be long and boring. Since Michael left she talks to customers, plants and her cat, who begrudgingly tolerates it. Maybe it's time for a change. That manager job does not sound too bad. She loves to cook and being the manager of one of the busiest restaurants in town will get her out of the cocoon she is safely wrapped in. Besides it is more money—a no brainer!

The next day she accepts and becomes Queen of the Kitchen at the Tattered Jeans Bar and Grille, better known as the Scattered Genes at two in the morning.

The guy dishwashers are fun but the lone female never leaves dirty pots for the next day and the floor is always mopped. Cathleen bestows upon her the title of Princess Pearl Diver (PPD) since she already has the Queen title wrapped up. PPD is good for a few one-liners and girl talk after work.

Burgers are flying and potatoes popping on Saturday afternoon. Cathleen wonders what her second-in-command is doing and why he isn't at the grill. Cathleen calls out to Kiwi, the assistant cook. "Where's your neck?" as she sees his bushy head pop through the swinging doors. Since everyone is forever asking Kiwi where his brains are, this is a refreshing approach and it sticks. Cathleen has started something—soon everyone in Crested Butte is asking, "Where's your neck?" in reference to any and all applicable acts of stupidity.

She thinks back now to those days—a strange time to have these memories return as she is wheeled down the hallway on a gurney. She and The Princess became lifelong friends. Her girlfriend will wait while she has the procedure and then drive her back home. They have come a long way since those days at the Tattered Jeans. Her girlfriend has been through some rough times and she has struggled getting her comedy act up and running, but they are both doing well now. Flashes of phone calls from the Midwest, where her friend moved to after her first disastrous marriage to Gracie's father, go drifting across her mind like a TV trailer. She sure went through a nasty breakdown and after recovering she jumped too fast into another marriage. I tried to slow her down but her urge to be settled just outweighed any reason. Gary was a nice guy but they were badly suited, so, after six years, they parted ways. Boy, a lot of life happened over those years.

In an anesthesia haze, thoughts about her own relationships slip in and out—they all seem to have heated up and burned out quickly except for Michael. She just wasn't enough to keep him from his urges to document lives in places like New Zealand and Sri Lanka. His photography is exceptional. Occasionally, she sees it in travel magazines. After fifteen years she still listens for phone calls in the night from halfway around the world. Her brief thing with Marty made her sad. That could have been something if his drinking had not sent her away. She wonders if she could have saved him. The sedative slowly takes her thoughts, allowing her to drift off after them.

Maggie sits in the wooden chair in the corner of a room with a control panel, TV screwed to the wall, sink in the corner and privacy curtain, and watches the clock. After Cathleen is wheeled out on the moveable bed she watches the procession of beds up and down the hall. One woman in particular keeps passing by, with first a full and then an empty bed. She wonders about their occupants: have they all been taken to a comedy club or the gas chamber? Who knows? She knows Cathleen would prefer the gas chamber rather than the colonoscopy she is undergoing. It killed her mother, not the gas chamber, colon cancer, and so she must endure intimate probing in search of death polyps. Not that she would object to a little intimate probing but this was not what she had in mind.

The minutes click by in sixty flips of the skinny long hand. It is hypnotic and lulls her into thoughts of herself and Cathleen. First, the early days of partying at the Tattered Jeans, and making just enough money to ski and pay rent, then the next chapter of relationships, children and loss. They had lost parents, partners and, sadly, themselves. Now, in their fifties, they have at least found themselves, although physically they are experiencing new losses like hearing and bladder control. They use laughter like a hanky to catch life's overspills.

They are working together again, not in a restaurant, though. No, her dishwashing days ended quite some time ago. Now they manage a small bookstore. She and Cathleen pooled their savings and got a small business loan to open a bookstore in the downtown area. It was her dream but it is Cathleen who keeps it going with her warmth and sense of humor. Customers come just to shoot the breeze with her and walk out with a book they probably hadn't intended to buy. On Wednesday evenings Cathleen does a free comedy bit in the store; it brings in a crowd and gives her a chance to practice her material. Being a stand-up comedian in a small city does not pay the bills but Cathleen loves it. Even if they don't move a lot of books on comedy night, it does cause a run on lattes and espressos.

The wonderful window arrangements and children's programs are the outpouring of Cathleen's whimsical nature. They lure shoppers to her web and she does the rest. Maggie knows she is the business end of things. She keeps the books and inventory while Cathleen keeps the customers coming. They are a good team.

Soon Cathleen rolls back in, slightly groggy and grinning. The nurses check vitals and give her some juice. She grimaces. "Gas," she says. "I feel like someone hooked a helium tank to my ass and opened the valve."

Dr. Carson swoops into the room. "How's it going?"

Cathleen manages a smile but it fades quickly.

"Gas?" he asks. She nods. "Get in touch with your masculine side: Let it rip!" he grinningly goads her." Go ahead, pull my finger." The room erupts in laughter.

After getting dressed, Cathleen walks slowly to her friend's car.

"When is your next gig?" her friend asks.

"Not till Saturday night so I can lay around for a day or two."

"Where's it at?"

"I'm working the Hilton for some kind of convention, I forget what kind."

"Have you worked up your routine or are you using the one from that last benefit you did?"

The anesthetic still floating around in her brain causes Cathleen to pause a moment. "Oh, yeah. I have some new stuff to add to the benefit stuff I did."

Her friend laughs. "That stuff you did at the benefit was a hoot. I just loved it."

Cathleen bends over and holds her stomach.

"More gas?"

"Yep."

"This experience should certainly give you lots of material for your act."

"Oh yeah, it's doing that. I think maybe I should ask Dr. Carson to be my straight man. He's a funny guy."

Interlude XII

"...and to conclude, David's other sister, Laney, will read a list of things the couple share a love for."

- Rivers, canyons, mountains and deserts
- John Denver songs and Terry Tempest Williams' *Red*
- Glasses of wine and starry nights on the deck
- Dancing in the kitchen to Frank and Neil
- Cuddling on the couch
- Gatherings with family and friends
- Fear of time passing and the joy of waking to each other
- Writing and reading by the fireplace
- Respect for each other's solitude
- *Red Violin,* their favorite movie
- Hikes at 13,000 ft
- Margaritas in the desert
- The Tao te Ching
- Willingness to laugh at themselves
- Reading the Sunday morning paper in bed
- The Spirit of Life
- Each other

25

flesh

O de to joy! the tiny fingers, I remember them holding on so fiercely; you hold on still, sometimes too tight, I want to say, let go and trust, trust that the right thing will happen—it is the Tao, you know; there is still something indescribable living within me—it's you; birth does not expel the body that it once housed, it only transforms it; you breathe air now and grow, beautiful and strong; your wit keeps two old souls from drifting into stale; those eyes the color of the Colorado sky, giggle, like the preteen they once guided; braided and headbanded you hiked grandly over the canyon's wire mesh bridges, clinging to my backpack, but determined to please me; you please me with every breath, I require nothing more.

SHE WONDERS WHY HER HEAD FEELS SQUEEZED and her arms have no room to move. Her knees are tucked up almost to her chin. She tries to stretch out but her head pushes up against a hard surface and her feet push out but there is little give at that end too. She strains again to expand. Voices murmur in the distance. It is dark and she so badly wants out of this place. Again and again she pushes against the barrier. She is making some progress, she thinks, as she feels her head move, not much, but it moved something. Again, the voices, one quiet, calm, and one sharp and frantic. The sequence repeats and again she feels her head move. There is a loud gasp and she sees light, she is upside down looking at the world from between two pillars. The light hurts her eyes and she screams. Soon her arms and legs are freed. Someone wraps her in a blanket and holds her. The stark air hits her lungs; surprised, she screams again.

It's 4:15 A.M., a man's voice shouts "It's a girl!" There is a bunch of cheering.

Soon she falls asleep in the arms of a woman whose voice she knows but whose face is not too clear.

The young mother stares into the bassinet at her tiny baby girl. They name her Grace for the light and beauty she brings to their lives. She places her hand on the baby's chest to assuage her fears and sometimes even pokes her awake when reason takes flight. Since she no longer believes that a god protects babies she knows she must do it herself. She keeps up this vigil night after night and nap after nap.

The early months are rough going; Grace has colic. Her young mother's nerves are shot; sleep deprived, she puts Grace in her crib and let's her cry for a while, picks her up, comforts her and tries again. When all else fails they visit a neighbor lady named Olive. The young mother guesses her to be in her eighties but is not sure. They become friends over their backyard gardens. Olive's is beautiful, so neat and full. Hers is withering, in need of attention, but the baby makes it difficult. Olive invites her over on afternoons when she appears most frazzled. She calms the baby while Mom chats away, lonely and alone all day. Olive guesses the husband works although they seem awfully poor. They become an odd sort of family. Olive's closest relatives are over an hour away, and she no longer drives, making it hard to see them. They have busy lives but make every effort to check on her and visit as much as possible. The young mother offers to mow the grass in return for some rattlesnake bean seeds. Olive is grateful; her joints cringe when she wheels the machine from its place in the garage. That used to be Albert's job. He has been gone eight years and still she misses him horribly. Those damn cigarettes were the death of him. God, how she wishes he would have quit sooner.

On Thanksgiving a blizzard hits and Olive's family is unable to come get her so she spends the holiday with her neighbor's family. It would have been lonely eating turkey by herself, staring at his empty chair.

On a rare afternoon the young mother finds herself with a sleeping baby and a few moments to herself. Her urge to write resurfaces from some region deep within the earth. After searching for a pen and paper she sits on the sofa and lets the words spill out.

> To Olive
> She lost her husband to smoking
> but still she kept the ceramic
> frog that puffed thinly
> on the tissue paper cigarette
> to amuse the crying toddler
> whose mother's nerves, stretched
> taunt by the rancor, slipped
> and loosened
> as tears dried to
> laughter.
>
> She tried hard not to remember
> the oxygen bottle and narrow
> tubes connecting his ears to
> disconnected lungs.
> The last year had been hard
> watching breath so taken for
> granted come like lottery
> winnings, in small amounts,
> never hitting the jackpot.
>
> Now grinning, the child cries
> "More" and she lights another

stick, the smoke curls out and
around to delight.

The vision of him in his chair,
smoke curling, warms and
chills her.

Funny how sad and happy
go together.

They move away when the baby is just a year old. The young mom calls occasionally and sends Christmas cards until the letter arrives telling her Olive has passed. She keeps a small china plate painted by Olive on display in her kitchen as a memorial to her kindness. She keeps a picture of Olive holding Grace on her mantel.

A SLENDER YOUNG WOMAN with iridescent blue eyes stares back at the camera and the eyes of her mother. The Grand Canyon provides the magnificent backdrop. The group gathering there begins to move slowly in the pre-dawn chill. They hoist their backpacks and sling them over one shoulder, then the other. They groan as the weight settles and adjust straps and belts. They are at seven thousand feet and have a long way to go. Their guide Morgan rounds them up for a group picture before they begin their descent.

This is her mother's dream: to hike the Grand Canyon before senility or incontinence set in. Grace's plan was to go to Mexico over spring break but that fell through so she called her mom and offered to accompany her into the canyon. They signed up for a woman's backpacking trek through the Grand Canyon Institute because private permits were not available the week of her spring break.

The group had gotten together the day before to meet, assess their gear and ready their packs. It is a diverse group ranging in age from twenty (Grace) to a sixty-year-old from California. There are eight of them including the guide.

In headband with braids flapping, Grace starts down the trail. Water bottles clipped on D-rings bounce as their feet carry them down to the bowels of the earth, or so it seems. Hour after hour passes by with little conversation; Grace and Maggie lead the way. At forty-seven her mom is still in good shape and they both hit the gym hard in the months preceding the trip. The views from the top are spectacular but distant. The actual moving into the arteries and veins of the canyon takes on a new dimension. Like that old movie *Fantastic Voyage* where they shrunk down some scientists and inject them into a human, she feels like she is entering the inner workings of the earth. The geology is inconceivable, millions of years, ocean bottom, upheavals and shifts all conspiring to create this land of rock and river. Like dichotomous elements they define each other, each shaping the other. They stop to rest about halfway down and let the back of the pack catch up.

Grace feels a chill as she slips her pack off her sweaty back. So far so good, she thinks as she surveys her body parts. Her feet are fine, the one part that concerned her. She chose tennis shoes and is happy with her choice. Beef jerky and trail mix along with some big chugs of water and a potty break and they are back on the trail. Once again, she and her mom forge ahead. Strange that the worst part of the hike so far has been the mule piss. It seems mules, being of pack mentality, must pee right where the last one has creating lakes of urine, which must be navigated cautiously. God, what a smell! Not to mention the fact that you, as hikers, must yield the right-of-way to the lazy bastards sitting on mule back. Time and again they plaster themselves to the cliff bank while the heavy-laden beasts of burden enjoy the width of the trail. Grace cannot help but think that the mules should not be allowed; somehow it violates the sanctity of place. In order to show proper dignity and respect, your feet must touch the surface and your body connect with the canyon's soul through sweat and sinew. She would make an exception for the physically challenged individual but the rest should be relegated to the Rim to snap a few pictures and head to the souvenir shop to complete their experience.

Grace and her mom reach the bottom just after noon. Soon the small beach is littered with packs, shirts, shoes and socks. In sports bras and shorts they plunge into the river, shrieking as the just-above-freezing water encompasses them. Refreshed, they stretch out like lizards in the sun, books in hand. Who needs Mexico? It is another almost two hours before the last of the group arrives; they collect their gear and head to their group camp site. There are metal containers for all the food items. It seems they have militia-trained rodents who can pretty much get into all but the most secure containers. Grace learns the hard way as her packages of oatmeal, inadvertently left in the pocket of her backpack hanging from a wire six feet off the ground, fall victim to the stealthy creatures.

The first night around the campfire they get to know one another. Morgan, the guide, is from Colorado and teaches geology at Mesa State College when she is not guiding; Carrie, aged thirty-five, is single and has just left the National Guard where she had served since high school. Allysia is forty, an artist, married with two grown children; Janet, thirty-one, lives with her cats and is an information technology contractor; Sandra, fifty-one, is an aging earth mother who, with her biker boyfriend, owns a health food store in northern California; and Joan, the sexagenarian, enjoys her grandchildren and her work as a librarian. All had dreams of making this trip; this is the thread that binds them. Only Janet's spirit seems ill at ease in this setting. Constant complaints grate on the other members' nerves but each in turn quiets their minds so as not to miss the more subtle messages of place. Not given the attention she craves, Janet slowly slips into the background, pouting as she goes.

Ah, the camaraderie of pain. Groans can be heard the next morning as each camper crawls from their tent. Overnight some evil magic has shortened their calf muscles by an inch, making each step excruciating. One by one they hobble to the facilities, begging for relief and cursing their bodies.

Grace and her mom pass on the day's scheduled hike in order

to sunbathe and veg out with a good book. Both have learned the lesson of less is more. A vacation must include some rest and relaxation, so although they are certain the hike will be as beautiful as described, they are dedicated to their premise and stroll to the beach, lotion and book in hand. Grace reads Barbara Kingsolver's *Prodigal Summer*, her mom reads *The Best of Edward Abbey*. She loves his irreverence and staunch defense of the desert southwest. Ed would cry if he could see the development at the Rim and the Phantom Ranch at the canyon's bottom—maybe he did and that's why he died so young. Her mom shares excerpts from his book. This one is from *Journey Home* and is entitled "The Great American Desert":

> ...Survival Hint #1: Stay out of there. Don't go. Stay home and read a good book, this one for example...
> ...let me enumerate the hazards. First the Walapai tiger, also known as conenose kissing bug... The kissing bug is fond of warmth and like Dracula requires mammalian blood for sustenance... Selecting a tender point, the bug slips a conical proboscis into your flesh, injecting a poisonous anesthetic... If you are of average sensitivity to a kissing bug's poison your entire body breaks out in hives, skin aflame from heel to toe.

After that Ed goes on to warn of rattlesnakes, centipedes, millipedes, tarantulas, black widows, brown recluses, coral snakes, Gila monsters and giant hairy scorpions, not to mention the sun. Sunstroke, heatstroke and dehydration he recounts as common and sometimes fatal misfortunes.

"However," her mom says, "my favorite Ed Abbey line about the desert goes as follows: "It has been said, and truly, that everything in the desert either stings, stabs, stinks or sticks."

So why are we here? She wonders. For the same reason Ed was driven to live in a spider and snake infested trailer under the blazing sun—for the desert's indescribable beauty and the sense of order amongst the chaos of the human spirit. We are centered, alert, and alive in its presence. It washes us clean of the detritus of civilized society and we are primal/primate again, back to our natural state, raw and exposed to the elements.

The hike back up to the Rim is done over two days. Half-way up, they stay at the Bright Angel Campground and finish the hike the next day. Smelly and depleted Grace and her mom reach the top of the Rim forty-five minutes ahead of the next hiker in the group. They hitch a ride back to the general store to purchase beer and then head to the hotel. The first beer goes down extremely fast and smooth. They draw straws for who gets the first shower; Grace wins and does not surface for thirty minutes. The hot water pelting down is indescribably wonderful. After her mom's turn they both empty one more beer and succumb to the exhaustion in their muscles. Several hours later her mom awakens and watches her sleeping daughter. She thinks back to that tiny infant in the crib and checks to see that her chest is moving. That evening after a meal of steaks and a few glasses of wine they call it a day. The next morning they pack up the car amidst occasional groans from aching muscles and sadly say good-bye to the most incredible hole in the ground. Time to go home.

Twenty-five years later, the thought of ever losing her daughter still cripples her; she chases it out with a pitchfork whenever it appears. She fears that if her daughter ever quit breathing, so, too, would she, as though their autonomic systems share some kind of common control. Daily phone calls confirm her daughter's continued breathing. She has learned the fragility of life, the randomness of loss and the beauty of every day.

26

magenta

You may be the toughest and the easiest to draw; nights at the Silver Dollar shooting pool and driving the bases at the high school in your jeep, the sheriff asking us to go home—too much fun; you were the impetus behind the greatest change in my life, now we paint waterfalls and mountains and drink dry martinis—clinky tinky!! kayaking down the river of life we talk about everything; your life is one big dream from anyone else's point of view, you DO! hiking and rafting the grand canyon, trips to aruba for gambling, new york's finest broadway plays, piano and planting, swinging your clubs till the snow flies then turning them into skis; you have lived five normal people's lifetimes; from you I learned to follow my path courageously, outrageously and to eat and drink deeply of life; carpe diem, latin for you.

SYDNEY TAKES HER GLUE-SPATTERED PANTS, chipped nails, dry and cracking fingers, aching back and knees back to her cabin. It was finally done. Before leaving she applied a last coat of floor wax and stood smugly in the doorway admiring the masterpiece, twelve hundred square feet of tile, start to finish in five days. Sydney and her partner tore out the old stuff, installed new sub floor and tiled their asses off—two staircases and a sunken living room. Whew!

Looking at her grout-caked nails she has to chuckle. She is a long way from New York's finest restaurants and the University of Maryland where she graduated with a master's degree in anthropology. The Hunter's Country Club where Sydney learned to play tennis and golf comes back to her like episodes of the *Twilight Zone*. Had she really lived that life? Her parents, Irv and Esther, supported her need to leave and make it on her own. She could have easily lived on their money but that would have sucked the life out of her.

It was a crazy cross-country trip after college that landed her in Colorado and a job installing ceramic tile. She had let her fingers do the walking on a map and pointed her car wherever the chosen destination turned out to be. She still sojourns, yearly, back East, to fulfill her need for Broadway plays and family visits. Her brothers, as available, join her in a week of skiing and debauchery each winter. They, too, marvel at her adventurous spirit and chide her good-naturedly about her rustic living conditions.

Sydney invites her tiling partner back to her cabin for a celebration dinner. They each grab a shower and a glass of wine. Steaks are put on the grill and potatoes in the oven.

With dinner and a second bottle of wine done, the conversation turns to the future. Their bones are communicating with their brains through the wine saying, "We can't do this for forever, maybe not even another year." "So," Sydney says, "if there is one thing in your life you could do, what would it be?"

Her partner's answer comes out before the question mark can be perceived. "I'd go back and finish college!"

"Well, why don't you?"

MAGGIE IS BACK IN COLLEGE by the fall. She calls Sydney at least once a month and visits when she has a break. Sydney can see the toll the stress of classes, a child, a part-time job and an unemployed husband is having on her friend. She wishes she could do something but she is busy keeping her own head above water. Her friend has always been thin but she is gaunt and grey. She hopes she makes it to graduation in one piece.

    Sydney's cabin in the woods is her refuge. A river runs just to the west, lulling her with baby gurgles. Flowers inhabit every square inch not taken up by the vegetable garden. The smell of pine trees arrives with the sunlight through the kitchen window as she sips her first cup of coffee each morning. The blue sky overhead is so intense it shakes the sheets out in her head and freshens her thoughts. It's a happy place and fits her like her favorite sweats. She hibernates these days except for trips to exotic places. Her old tile partner visits occasionally. In fact, she will be coming in on Friday to celebrate her new career.

27

wheat

Best mentor, mature and caring beyond all other friends, visited me in the hospital when I crashed during my last semester at college, no one else would; from you I learned to teach and believe in myself.

CAROL SITS IN THE WAITING ROOM of the psychiatric wing of Community Hospital. She wonders how her best research assistant ended up here. On a bad day her assistant accomplished more than most of the rest of the crew on their best days. She knew her life was rough, an ugly divorce, a young child to support and financial difficulties, but she seemed to be handling it just fine. They had talked briefly about what was happening and it just did not add up to voluntary commitment. There must be more, she thinks.

THE SCISSORS AND KNIVES in the kitchen drawers have hands that reach into her thoughts. Carol's assistant sits on the toilet having locked the bathroom door to keep them from finding her. Will they harm her or her daughter? She doesn't want to know. Maybe she should throw out all the sharp things in the house to stop them from haunting her waking dreams. Sweat runs down her forehead and her hands vibrate. Crazy, she's going crazy is the thought that worms its way into her consciousness. She wishes she could call Jarrad but it's two o'clock in the morning. Curling up on the bathroom rug, she cries herself into a ragged sleep.

Carol's assistant lies curled in fetal position in the corner of her therapist's office, terrified of everyone and everything. Jarrad, her therapist, stares from across the room. "Do you need a rest?" he asks.

"Yes," she mumbles, unable to meet his eyes with hers—they are fixed on the back of her head. He dials the phone and makes the arrangements.

After signing all the papers, she is taken to a room with two single beds and a nightstand. She climbs under the covers, pulls them to her chin and sleeps—her first undisturbed sleep in weeks. She is safe here, ashamed but safe. The morning orderly arouses her from dreamless sleep. "Time for breakfast and then group," She moves in slow motion, her brain numbingly serene—no worries. In group, they poke and prod the flimsily sealed wound. She has just managed to staunch the bleeding. "It's too soon," she says.

The therapist looks away in agreement and directs the question to the woman twisting dyed red hair. "Why are you here?"

"My children think I am crazy because I am spending their expected inheritance," she replies. Everyone nods in sympathy.

Slowly the young assistant allows a thought in—how DID I get here? Overwhelmed, she folds the question back up and sticks it back in her pocket to be examined another day.

Evelyn sits next to her at lunch. "Hi, new girl, what brings you to Le Spa de Loco? The manicure, pedicure, massage... maybe it's the gourmet cuisine? Ah that's it." She glances down at a plateful of brown stuff and manages a feeble grin. They are soon talking about their children, family, and friends, anything but the cuckoos who hide behind boulders in their brains. After finishing lunch they head off to their occupational therapy session.

Just like the Shel Silverstein children's poem, "the Whatifs," her thoughts come creeping in as she crawls into the sheets. It is unfair that they strike at that most vulnerable moment, when the darkness without closes in on the darkness within, she thinks.

She wakes the next morning slightly disoriented. It takes a few moments to remember where she is and then a few more for anxiety to begin its march through her veins. In session today she is not given a reprieve but must start to engage emotionally. The story of her disastrous marriage and the destruction of trust fueled her downward spiral. She began questioning every word from his mouth. The depression and anxiety deepened with each new round of lies, each phone call from a creditor he said he had paid, each bounced check at the grocery store. Looking back over the signs, her self-loathing peaked. How had she been so gullible and naïve? Leaving overwhelmed her, staying would destroy her, so she did nothing for too long. She manages to detail the insomnia, run-on sentences in her brain that she cannot turn off, the sweats, fears of pretty much everything. Even to herself she sounds crazy. This is breakdown number two. She worries about her daughter but knows she is in good hands at her in-laws. Rosie and Richard are good people and love both her and her daughter. The therapist thanks her for sharing and the group nods its sympathy. Lunch is the same as yesterday and in the afternoon she finishes her clay pot in occupational therapy. Back in her room she is surprised to be summoned to the visiting room.

The door opens and her assistant hesitates before entering the visiting room. Carol is afraid she will retreat but watches as she takes a seat opposite her. She looks even thinner than before, like more life has leaked out of her.

"You didn't need to come," her assistant says in greeting.

Carol is not sure how to reply but finally says, "I wanted to, to see if you needed anything or if I could do something, help out. How are you doing?"

Her assistant considers a sarcastic response like "C'mon, look at me. I'm in the loony bin" but knows Carol's concern goes deeper and answers honestly.

"I'm scared that I might never be right again, that my wiring has gotten so mixed up that they won't be able to untangle it. I'm relieved and embarrassed to be here. I suppose I'm the talk of the lab, crazy old whatshername."

Carol's stomach lurches as she remembers how close she came to the edge a few years ago. "You know almost everyone has come close to being where you are and some have even visited a place like this. It happens to a lot of people. Most of your colleagues have stepped quickly back to shore off of thin ice; some have fallen in but they have all returned and so will you. You need to take care of yourself, give yourself time. You'll heal."

She did not know if Carol was just saying those things to be kind but she feels a small sense of strength enter her muscles and mind. She needs not to feel so alone and scared.

Carol fills her in on the day-to-day stuff in the lab and they joke about the less than discreet liaison between one of the bosses and his administrative assistant, an inside story amongst their group. Carol looks at her watch.

"Time to get going. The kids will be home from soccer practice and be starving, as they say. You take care," accompanies a kiss on the cheek and hand squeeze. Her assistant smiles and waves. Both pretend not to see the tears run down her cheek.

At home that night Carol thinks back to a time in her life where she skirted the edge. A failed relationship sent her reeling too. All her self-doubt that had waited in the closet while she clothed herself in his self-esteem came back to assault her when she had to return the borrowed image. She had lived vicariously through his good looks and self-assurance. Why had she not seen it then? How blind to herself she was, how clueless? Guy had swept into her life and taken command and she let him. That is the part that bothers her most. Why was she so eager to give up control? She feels the anger rise again, a bit muted, but still there. What in her had her seeking an alter ego? She is left with so many questions and a fear of the answers.

While wrapped up in Guy she withdrew from friends and family. The guilt still lives in her. Why had he taken his life and why did she not see it coming? The loss of Aaron, her twin brother, haunts her. The person she shared the womb with did not share his anguish and fears, his fears of losing the love of his family if they knew. There was the young man, handsome in his dark suit, standing in the back at the cemetery, tears rolling down his cheeks. He came up to her afterwards and introduced himself. He said his name was Peter and that he was Aaron's partner for the last five years. Peter sobbed as he confessed to pushing Aaron to tell his family about them. He did not know the conflict would send him over the edge.

Carol wonders how she could have been so self-absorbed to have not seen her brother's inner struggle. In their youth they finished each other's sentences and read each other's thoughts. What happened? She was so wrapped up in Guy and the fairy-tale relationship that she lost touch with herself, her family and her friends. God, how she hated women who did that and there she was standing chest deep in the waters of self-fascination. The guilt, self-loathing, insecurity and disgust overwhelmed her in the aftermath of the break-up and the loss of her brother left a black hole inside her. The hollowness echoed as emotions were sucked into the void.

She is not going to abandon Maggie, not like she abandoned her brother.

Interlude XIII

"...Next we have a reading of poems. The first is a poem David wrote to Maggie for their engagement, it is read by David's niece."

*Near-canyons folded stone
that guides and stirs my soul,
on wings of wrens are carried
fates echoes, fates summoned toll...*

*Wished to leaves though written
in copper's cobbled stream,
words found in cascades hidden
wake to rouse my dream...*

*A stir from scarlet shadows
lace unraveled shawl
esses over stone
silent colors fall...*

*Spired towers grace
tethered to the sky
drums my breathing heart
giving me this day...*

*Darting wrens
that hem the curtained walls
choirs my spirits
wanting to love you,
my Maggie
most, most of all.*

28

white

I encountered you many times throughout my life, you were there in the rain in Glenwood Canyon, you were there on a deserted highway in the midwest, we met again in the Plaza de Blanc in New Mexico and again at Chaco Canyon, the ancestors, father sky, mother earth, great spirit, god; you are all these things and so much more, in the darkness you shine a light, when the world shakes, your arms steady; your hands reach down from the clouds and embrace, I breathe you in over and over and am healed.

ESPERANZA DEPUY SITS IN THE BUS TERMINAL in some western Colorado town where she is changing buses, shopping bag at her knee. She scans the terminal, red eyes and unwashed hair in abundance. She pulls her bag closer. The smells are worse than the visuals. Urine predominates followed close by body odor and stale beer. She consults her watch, still fifteen minutes till they board. A rack of brochures of places these people will never see sits next to Esperanza. She takes one down and peruses it. Visit Colorful Moab is its cover headline with pictures of red rock monuments and brightly colored jeeps driving up steep trails. Esperanza wonders why people have to drive in these beautiful places. Can't they just get out and walk and really get the taste and feel of the place. The world scares her sometimes, too much noise and motion;

people seem to have forgotten how to sit quietly and observe. Now it is stimulate me, entertain me, and bring the world to me, rather than using your imagination to entertain yourself and going out into the world to explore. She worries about her grandchildren in a world of material goods calling to them to fulfill needs like self-esteem, which cannot be gained from owning something or wearing the right clothes but which must be earned through experience, through challenging themselves and, win or lose, gaining knowledge about who they are and what they are made of. They have lost the old ways; they are restless as the stories are told and have forgotten the ancestors and their powers.

The PA system announces her bus and Esperanza rises to board. A young woman bumps into her as she picks up her bag.

"Oh, excuse me, I'm so sorry," the young woman apologizes as she reaches out to steady the older woman.

"That's okay, I'm fine," Esperanza replies as she catches her balance.

"I hate these bus stations, they give me the creeps. The strangest people seem to travel by bus. Have you ever seen so many tattoos and scars on men?" the young woman rambles on nervously.

"No, I haven't," Esperanza replies. "It does seem to attract some wayward characters."

"Where are you going?" the young woman asks.

"I'm going to Chicago to visit my daughter. She lives on the twenty-seventh floor of one of those high-rise buildings on Lake Shore Drive. I'll see Lake Michigan for the first time and we're going to shop at Water Tower Place. It's exciting and a little frightening," Esperanza confides, surprised at how easy it is to talk to this stranger. They agree to sit together to avoid having to sit with any of the other passengers.

After boarding the bus and getting situated, Esperanza glances over at her new travel companion. She has a sad face, too sad for a person her age; a face like that comes only with many years of struggle and disappointment. There is a nervousness about her too, tension in the position of her shoulders and lines of her face.

Sometimes, when we are young, we have such seriousness that only age teaches us is foolish. She can tell that the young woman has retreated into her mind, so Esperanza chats with the bus driver. She asks how long he has been driving and he replies, "Thirty years next week."

"Wow, that's a long time," she responds.

"Yeah, I'm thinking about calling it quits. Nowadays, all this drug stuff, I got to worry every day what kind of crazy I'm gonna git on my bus. Used to be just a bunch of drunks who slept most of the time and didn't give me no trouble, but not anymore. These crazy kids get on the bus, all hopped up on something, and I got to watch my back. It's just getting to be too much. I ain't no young man anymore." Esperanza commiserates about the state of today's youth while her companion appears to sleep.

The young woman stares out the window through her left eye, keeping the right one closed to appear asleep. She does not want to talk. They clear the town limits and head north to pick up I-70. More small towns roll by framed by a colorless sky. The grey outside matches her grey insides. She has failed, failed at so many things. Her choice of men led her to a disastrous marriage. Charming and manipulative, he kept her guessing about his behavior and where the money went. She finally caught him lying, cheating and stealing, confirming all of her suspicions. How had she been so gullible? How had she given him ten years of her life? There were many signs she had ignored until she stood teetering on the edge of a black hole. Her crushed soul sits in her suitcase with a pair of blue jeans, some t-shirts and the necklace that belonged to her dead mother. She cherishes it for some reason, even though it is worthless; one tiny chip of diamond on the end of the initial. How clever she once thought herself to be and how stupid she is in reality. Severe poverty and the strange voices running nonstop like a television banner along the bottom of the screen in her head put her on that bus. After years of lies and self-deceit she could no longer control the ramblings in her mind. The medications they gave her in the hospital do not work all that well.

Exercise is the only thing that calms her mind but she can not run twenty-four hours a day.

The bus stops at a small mall in Glenwood Springs for lunch. Esperanza joins the other passengers in the café, where she orders a grilled cheese sandwich. Her companion wanders off into the mall after smoking a cigarette.

The young woman pauses in front of a bookstore and slowly enters. She wanders through each aisle, not really looking for anything in particular. Each of the book covers vie for her hand. Most marketing people do not know depression; they use too much color. Depression seeks grey. Her eyes come to rest on a white book with black lettering *Coping with Depression: A Woman's Book of Hope*. She picks it up and thumbs through it. As she reads a few brief passages, she sees herself on the pages. There it is—the name, address and phone number of her lost soul. All of her symptoms—malaise, tastelessness, futility, fear, and anxiety—spring from the pages. She puts the book back on the shelf; six dollars is more than she can spare. Maybe she can get to a library and check out a copy when she gets to her sister's.

In a sunken state, she re-boards the bus. Esperanza feels her sadness wrap around her shoulders like a shawl. She reaches out to touch the young woman's arm, wanting to comfort her.

"Life is difficult sometimes, yes?"

The young woman stiffens slightly at Esperanza's touch and then the words come pouring out.

"Sometimes much more difficult than one person can take. I've messed up my life so badly and wasted so many years. Why did I let him drag me down and do things I'm ashamed of? I became the very person I never wanted to be. I let myself think being a victim was a way of life instead of just something to rise above. Why was I so gullible? Why didn't I fight back and do what I knew was right? No, I just followed the herd down the wrong path and have only myself to blame. I could've said no, I could've left a long time ago, but there I was, chasing down drugs at two in the morning, just like him. When I couldn't beat him, I joined him. This was not the life I intended to live. I was going to be a teacher, marry a nice man and have children. How in the hell did I let myself get drawn so off course? I don't even know how to go back and find myself, I lost me so many years ago. I feel sick thinking about who I've become. It's hard to get out of bed and see my face in the mirror. How do I find all the pieces and re-arrange them so that the outcome is different next time? I don't know where to start, I feel so overwhelmed."

The young woman starts shaking and then sobbing. Esperanza puts her arm around her, and, with her free hand, digs in her bag.

"Here," she says, "this book has helped me many times."

Maggie just stares at the book, *Coping with Depression—A Woman's Book of Hope*.

Esperanza holds her as her body expels pent-up emotion, tears stream down her face. When she is able to exert some control, the young woman looks into Esperanza's rich dark eyes and thanks her profusely. Esperanza hands her a hanky to wipe her face and says to keep it as she may need it again.

As the bus sways through Glenwood Canyon, the young woman reads the book and cries. The book and the hanky serve the same purpose—they wipe the blur from her vision. The streams of tears down her cheeks meander like the Colorado River outside the window. As she pauses to absorb what she is reading, she remembers that the Great Divide directs the flow of the rivers and knows that the Great Divide in her soul directs the flow of tears from her ducts. As they wind their way down into Denver, the book continues to tell her that she is not alone and that her "Great Divide" will heal.

Esperanza and the young woman sit together in the Denver bus terminal, waiting for the next bus to Chicago. The young woman scans the eyes of the strangers; most are dulled by too much—too much struggle, drugs, alcohol, life. She wonders if she looks the same to them. This is not a gathering of motivational speakers, she thinks, and chuckles to herself.

Esperanza and the young woman board the bus to their final

destination and settle in. The young woman pulls out the book and begins reading again. The book explains how low self-esteem, pent-up anger and frustration have led to a devastating depression. Her background had set her up to connect with a man who would only further her insecurities and provide opportunities for bad decisions. After discussing causes, the book describes what is needed to crawl out of the black hole. She will need a job, maybe teaching if she can handle it, and then a car and maybe even a house. It may be the flatness of Nebraska or sheer exhaustion, or maybe the hope that tomorrow really will be a better day, but whatever it is, it lulls her into her second thoughtless sleep in months.

The bus pulls into the Chicago depot at two-thirty in the afternoon, thirty-five minutes late. Esperanza shakes the young woman's shoulder to awaken her. She sits up, rubs her eyes and smiles.

"Wow, how long have I been sleeping?" she asks.

"Since Lincoln, Nebraska, I think."

"Holy cow, that was a long time," the young woman says with surprise.

They both smile. In the terminal they hug good-bye.

"Thank you so much for this book," the young woman says again. "Are you sure you don't want it back? I can get another copy."

"No, you keep it. It's been good to me and now it will be good to you. Adiós, mi amiga. Vaya con diós."

Esperanza turns to look for her daughter, who is running across the terminal to greet her. The young woman spots her sister Jackie and her daughter Grace, who has been staying with Jackie until she could wrap things up in Colorado. Hugs and kisses are shared all around. She is not alone anymore.

29

rust

You were not the best therapist, but you knew something of damaged human beings, you knew resolution or closure was needed, you taught me it was okay to yell at the dead.

LINDA HAS HAD A LONG UPHILL BATTLE with an abusive father. It's what drove her to become a therapist. Over and over again he reinforced his messages: "You're so stupid a rat has a higher IQ. You ain't never done nothin right. You cain't cook, clean, sew, iron my shirts or make a bed worth a shit." He repeated these daily, like a mantra. A B at school sent him into a tirade of how she was wastin her time on schoolin'. She wore the bruises like war wounds but without the pride. She avoided him as best she could, hiding out in her bedroom or the library. Whenever she was forced to converse with him she cringed. He made her beg for every little thing and enjoyed watching her squirm. She remembers needing feminine products and his furious face as he made her spell out the words. He worked at the steel mill as a foreman so he had plenty of experience with barking orders. Her mother died of cancer when she was ten years old. Somehow he blamed her.

Fortunately, a scholarship took her several states away; unfortunately his words followed her. She had trouble meeting new people because she feared everything coming out of her mouth sounded stupid; it also made it difficult to speak up in class for fear of looking foolish. As time went on she began to hear a new voice, her own, and decided that it really was not that bad. The one trait she could not shake was indecisiveness. Making her own decisions paralyzed her. It was junior year and time to declare a major. Her father demanded she stick to "women's work" like being a teacher or nurse, but that was not where her heart was. She wanted to help people like her, the ones who had been beaten up and down. Finally, after months of agonizing and several trips to the student counselor, she chose psychology. Her father threw a fit over the phone; she hung up on him. That was the last conversation they ever had. The next day a thirty foot I-beam swinging from a crane broke loose from its chain and crushed him.

In that crazy human psychotic way she mourned him with a mixture of relief and guilt. After all, he was her father, and didn't he provide the basics for her? She wept at his funeral and wondered why.

A YOUNG WOMAN SITS ON THE COUCH across from Linda. Like the country in 1929 she is in the grip of a great depression. Her psyche has suffered several wounds: years of unstable living, a marriage to an unbalanced personality and the loss of her mother who committed suicide.

"So, tell me about your mother. Were you close?"

"Yes and no. My mother was an unhappy person and when she inhabited that world she was distant and removed. When she emerged on occasion she could be wonderful and charming. She was a great cook and threw excellent parties — the Hostess with the Mostest as she liked to say. People gravitated to her in hopes of capturing some of her charisma. There was always anxiety about which Mother would greet me at the door each day after school — the one who had fried chicken on the stove or the one who was loaded on pills and booze. She didn't think we knew — but we did. All of us walked around it like a pile of shit on the lawn — we all saw it, no one wanted to touch it."

"Who found her?"

"I did. I was home from college for the weekend."

"How old were you?"

"Almost twenty. I got home and the house was unusually quiet, the TV was on but the volume was turned down, so I called out "Hi, Mom, I'm home." There was no response so I called again and again as I walked from room to room. I found her on her bed, vomit stuck in her hair. I shook her a couple times before realizing she wasn't breathing. I ran to the phone to call an ambulance. The paramedics tried to revive her but it was too late."

"What did you do while you were waiting?" Linda asks.

"I just sat there looking at her."

"Did you ever tell your mother how angry she made you? Did you ever tell her how pissed you were that she left you?"

"No, she was dead, so what was the point? She wasn't all bad, she did some good things."

Linda repeats her questions. "Have you ever told your mother how much damage she did to you, or how her dark moods affected you, or how her Jekyll and Hyde personality caused you to be anxious? How never having clean clothes and school supplies embarrassed and humiliated you?"

"No, no, I never did." She thinks back. When the darkness descended, her mother could be brutal. Every flaw would be pointed out in detail to show you just how ugly and useless you were. "Look at your skin, it's terrible. How will you ever get a man looking like that? And your hair looks like a rat's nest. Don't you ever comb it? Stand up straight, you're slouching again. You're getting a bit chunky these days. You'd better cut out the malts." It went on and on.

Linda sits quietly, waiting for her client to finish her thoughts.

"How do I tell her now?"

"Write her a letter. Put it all down, don't censor it. Let it all out, then go to the cemetery and read it to her, out loud. Yell if it makes you feel better. Don't worry, no one will hear. I know it sounds crazy but try it and let me know how you feel afterwards."

It does sound crazy and she doubts it will make any difference, however, in the end, she agrees to do it over the weekend and report back next week.

That Friday night she sits with pen and paper in her sparsely furnished living room. Her daughter is at a sleepover. She pulls an afghan over her legs and curls up on the couch. Their springer spaniel, Coffee, lies beside her as she writes. She gathers her thoughts while scratching Coffee's ears. Here goes, she thinks as she lowers her hand to the page. An hour and one-half later, she inhales deeply, massages her cramped hand and stretches out her legs. Ouch! They're stiff. She hobbles to the kitchen to refill her wine glass and returns to re-read her letter. She didn't know she had that much in her. She feels drained. A hot shower revives her and loosens up her achy joints. Tomorrow she will complete the task.

Saturday is a drizzly, midwestern October day. The wind whips in gusts through the deserted cemetery. Naked trees wrap branches around themselves as a shield against the damp and chill. It has been over ten years since she stood there as they lowered her mother's casket into the earth. She parks the car in front of the head stone that reads Loving Wife and Mother; a strangled laugh escapes her lips. With her collar pulled up against the damp wind she kneels near the stone bearing her mother's name; trembling, she unfolds the letter. She glances around to make sure she is alone before beginning.

Dear Mom,

It has been over ten years since you swallowed a bottle of Valium and chased it with a fifth of vodka. I found your cold body, stiff and lifeless. I was twenty. How selfish and cowardly an act. You probably knew I would be the one to find you. Was that your ultimate goal, to leave me with an everlasting image of your vomit-splattered face and hair, the one that would haunt my sleep for months? Maybe it is the penultimate complement to your Good Mother visage, crisp and clean, standing beside your masterpiece while the local reporters raved about your culinary talents. Even after eight children you looked good. I hid my ugly skin, tousled hair and slumped shoulders behind the garage and watched. You sent me to the store for groceries just so I would not embarrass you. How could someone who produced prize-winning entrees produce such ugly offspring? Hah! It was the gods conspiring to reach your soul but you kept it shrouded.

Maybe if you had seen beyond the surface of things you would have seen me for more than a poor reflection of yourself. I lived in constant anxiety of having you discover new infractions and greater unworthiness in me. How many ways could I displease you? Let me count the ways: poor skin, messy hair, ghastly posture, slovenly habits, shy responses, tomboy tendencies, the list goes on. I am not ugly, chunky and slouched over. I have beautiful blue eyes, chestnut hair and a heart yearning to love. I received an award at school for working with physically-challenged students but you were to drunk to attend. I was a member of the National Honor Society and vice-president of my senior class. You cared little for this unless you were crowing to your friends as though it was your accomplishment, not mine. All honor and glory be to thee! I am somebody in spite of the fact that you treated me like nobody. I have friends who love and respect me and, in return, I them. I graduated from college. I am somebody!

I hate all the times I came home to you passed out in your bed, smelling of liquor, stinking of vanity, and then pretending it never happened. I don't think you fooled as many people as you thought you did. The neighbors knew, I'm sure they heard the fights. I never brought friends home after school because I never knew which mother would open the door.

And who were you? I used to pity you, I had learned in school that drug and alcohol addiction was a disease. I tried to view you with compassion, to understand your sickness, but, in the end, it was your character that was corroded. With or without the addiction you needed to put me down to feel better about yourself. You destroyed your child to feed your ego. How in the hell does that make you feel? Well, it made me feel like shit. Mission accomplished!

But in the end mostly what I hated was that you left me. I needed you to be my mom. I needed someone to call when I was homesick away at college. I needed someone to send me little care packages. I needed someone to ask about men and relationships. And I still do. I am angry you were never that mom. I am alone and scared in a big world trying to figure things out for myself and failing miserably. Oh, not always, once in a while I get it right. There is no one to turn to who loves me unconditionally, who accepts me warts and all. Why was I not granted one of those mothers? I know that crap about that which does not kill us makes us strong and all the character-building stuff that's supposed to come out of adversity, but, quite honestly, it's a bunch of crap. All your mental and emotional insufficiencies only left me scarred. The strength I garnered was false strength, it was walls I built to protect myself which I am learning now must come down in order for me to find health. And the character building, oh yeah, I'm as sarcastic a character as there ever was. Again it protects me, something else I have to rid myself of — thanks. I'm doing a lot of rebuilding, the tearing down hurts, the building back up is daunting, but I will succeed because you failed. You failed to destroy me completely before you destroyed yourself. Again, thanks . . .

She stops for a moment to allow the throbbing in her head to subside. Her heart rate slows with a couple of deep breaths.

I do know one thing I learned from you: how not to treat my daughter. I will not pick at the loose chinks in her psyche, when she gets older, I will show her how to patch them herself and allow her the honor of having done it. I will respect her choices and support her right to make them. But mostly I love her

unconditionally. I tuck her in at night after reading a story, and play games in the day. We laugh and are silly together. I dry her tears and bandage scraped knees. I'm the same Mom each and every day; she can count on me. I don't use her for my own gratification. She'll grow to be her own person, strong in herself, kind, compassionate and whole.
Thanks!
Maggie

She folds the letter up and puts it back in her pocket while tears stream down her cheeks. She mourns the loss she never experienced and realizes that the person who gave her birth was only that, a receptacle. Her mother never embodied the spirit. Looking back now, she sees only a sad excuse for a human being, one whose own dysfunction fed the cycle. Well, she plans to break that cycle.

As she drives back to her apartment, something makes her pull off the road, get out of her car and dance in the rain—arms akimbo, legs doing a jig as the sun breaks through the clouds for the first time in three days. A passing motorist stares at her. She laughs.

On Wednesday, she reports her experience to Linda. She reads the letter to Linda and experiences nothing.

"How do you feel?" Linda asks.

"I don't know, lighter. The knots in my stomach have disappeared. I feel good."

"What now?"

"Well I was thinking about looking into a Masters' program at the university. My job will pay for it and maybe I'll buy the condo I've had my eye on, one with a backyard for our dog. Grace and I could really use more room too."

As they wrap up their session, Linda asks, "When do you want to come back?"

"I don't know. I feel pretty good right now so how about I call you if I need to talk?" Besides, she thinks, this is my life now, I'm going to live it.

"Okay, that works for me," Linda says through a slight grin.

Interlude XIV

"*...AND THEN A READING OF A POEM* written by Maggie to David, read by Maggie's niece."

Before You and I

Before you and I
A cup of coffee held my hand
At the opening notes of the sun's symphony

Before you and I
A blanket wrapped round my shoulders
As the night's breath hailed the moon's arrival

Before you and I
A wine goblet kissed my lips
As the fire leapt and danced in golden silhouette

Before you and I
I knew the loneliness of touch.

With you in my life I will know...
Hands hold
Arms enfold
Lips caress.

30

juniper

My need for perfection destroyed you; just like my parents, I was right and you were wrong, oh how habits become insidiously ingrained; I lost you but found something I so badly needed, I found a kinder gentler me inside a tough skin thickened by years of insecurity and defensiveness; time to strip a few layers, exposing softer tissue and vulnerability—a whole new world for me, no more defenses, I opened up to human foibles and self-laughter; from you I learned to be human, make mistakes, ask forgiveness, let go.

GARY STANDS IN THE KITCHEN staring at the woman he no longer wants, her blue eyes staring back at him, incredulously.

He repeats, "I'm leaving. I've given this a lot of thought. I'm sick of doing everything your way, never being right and feeling useless." She blinks several times; the words are still not registering. Leaving, what does he mean leaving?

"I'll call you in a couple of days to discuss the divorce."

DIVORCE! What is he talking about? They just celebrated their tenth anniversary with a trip to Barbados. They ate, drank, talked and made love all night. This just can not be happening. Gary picks up his bag and walks out the door. He feels a surge of power;

for once she does not get the last word. It feels good to see her speechless.

His wife stares at the door for what seems like hours but is only seconds and collapses on the floor, sobbing hysterically, feeling her heart pour out of her eyes. He can't just leave, she loves him; she can not function without him. With each new onslaught of thoughts she shakes harder and odd wrenching noises issue from her throat. She lies on the kitchen floor in a pool of tears and spittle; her eyes lock open until physical pain finally out-screams the emotional pain. She crawls to the couch and curls up in the fetal position. In the morning the face in the mirror frightens her so she shuts off the bathroom light and returns to the couch. At nine o'clock in the morning, the phone rings. She lets it. It rings again at ten and several more times throughout the day. She lets it roll to voice mail as she remains frozen under the afghan her grandmother crocheted. At seven o'clock in the evening, a loud rapping at the door rouses her from her stupor. She tries to ignore it but her sister's worried voice gives her the impetus to move. The look of shock on her sister's face confirms the mirror's view.

"What's wrong? What happened?"

"He's left" is all she can get out before her knees give out and her sister catches her.

"Who's left?" her sister says, still not comprehending the situation.

"Gary has left me," she chokes out through her hoarse vocal chords.

"Why?" The obvious question slips out before her sister can rein it in.

"Shit, if I knew why I probably wouldn't be here. I don't know… all he said… was something about… feeling useless and… then he walked out." She manages in between sobs and gasping for breath.

Jackie cradles her closely and rocks her gently. She shakes her head, trying to make sense of things. They seemed so happy. They were the one couple people were envious of; they laughed, played and finished each other's sentences. Slowly, her sobs give way to labored breathing and then silence.

"Have you eaten anything today?" Jackie asks as she helps her to a chair.

"No, I'm not hungry."

"Well, you need to eat something."

"Not right now, please. It would just make me sick."

"Okay, how about a cup of tea?"

"That's fine."

Her sister puts the cup in front of her with a slice of lemon on the saucer and joins her.

"What are you going to do?"

"I don't know. I don't even know where he is. He said he would call in a couple of days." She left out the part about the divorce. She just can not get her lips to say the word. This all feels so surreal, like being in a play about someone else's life.

"Your office called me today. They're worried about you."

"God, I can't go to work and act like nothing's happened. What am I going to do? There's just no way I'll be able to concentrate."

"It won't be good to sit here all alone," her sister counters.

The tears start up again, more of her strength draining out with each new bout.

"Maybe a shower will make you feel better," Jackie suggests after surveying her disheveled hair and swollen face.

"I can't, I can't go up to the bedroom. He's all over, his smell, his side of the bed, his half of the closet empty, his razor gone from the shower. I can't face it."

"Come stay with me tonight. I'll go pack some clothes for you and we can decide what to do in the morning."

On the third day, she makes it into the office. She gets there early, closes her door and stays there, intermittently crying and sorting through papers on her desk. A close colleague, Allysa, opens her door and sticks her head in—

"You okay?"

She keeps her swollen eyes down as she mumbles "Yes."

"Well, just let me know if you need anything."

"Sure." Somehow the word has gotten around but she is mostly grateful.

Her nerves are frayed waiting for Gary's phone call. The fourth and fifth days come and go, still no call. There are several hang-ups so maybe he is just getting his courage up. Finally, on Saturday afternoon she picks up the phone to find his voice at the other end.

"How are you?" he tries to say as casually as possible.

"Fine." Her emotions are bouncing from dread to elation and back. His voice, which has so often soothed her or made her laugh, sounds different.

"Can we talk?" she asked hesitantly.

"About what?" he says curtly.

Her mind is racing—what do you mean about what? About what's going on here, about why you walked out, about why you never told me you were unhappy, about why I'm getting hang up phone calls—this last one made her stomach flip.

"About us."

Gary does not want to talk; he always loses at that game.

"I don't think there's anything to talk about. I've made up my mind, I want a divorce." There is that word again, that incongruous word. It just does not fit, she thinks. They woke up Monday, drank coffee from the same carafe, kissed him good-bye and left for work, talked on the phone during the day, came home from work and he asked for a divorce. It just doesn't fit.

There is a long silence.

"How long have you been thinking about this?" she asks.

"A year, maybe more."

Silence again.

"Please don't do this," her voice cracks. "Can't we get help? This happens to lots of couples."

Gary is not going to get sucked in this time. "I'll have my lawyer send over the papers."

Lawyer, he has a lawyer, shrieks through her head. She hangs up; it is the only power she has left.

"Bitch!" he yells as he throws the phone across the room.

She sits with her head in her hands, sobbing again. It is amazing how much fluid the body can produce given the right stimulus. How can she go on? The sobbing accelerates until she stands retching over the toilet. There is nothing to lose because she has only consumed coffee all week. Every time she looks at food she gags. Her clothes are getting loose. Since coming home from her sisters, she sleeps on the couch in the family room, unable to face the bed. She does not know how not to rollover and reach for him in the night or kiss his grizzled chin upon waking. She shakes just entering the room to retrieve clean clothes. She moves her toiletries to the bathroom off the family room.

As word spread around the office, stares of compassion follow her down the hall. They leave her alone and take turns covering for her. She thanks them with her eyes, unable to speak the words without another flood of tears.

Two weeks later she arrives home to a large manila envelope in the mailbox. She freezes. The return address reads Harris, Harris and Lundberg, Attorneys-at-law. She can not go inside, taking with her a new life sentence, so she gets back in her car and begins driving aimlessly; first a right turn, then a left. The country roads are deserted, all the families home around their dinner tables. The tears start again; the rain on the windshield further distorts from blurred vision. She feels her heart being torn from her chest, a searing pain making it difficult to breathe. She accelerates faster and faster, rounding curves with tires slipping on wet pavement; the sound of gravel whaps in the wheel wells as she misses the edge of the road and slides off into a cornfield. Instinct takes over and she brakes the car to a halt a foot from a telephone pole. "I can't do this," she screams. "I can't take this." Over and over like a mantra, she murmurs, "Oh, God, please help me. She is not a religious person but she once heard that you should offer up your pain. There is nothing else she can do.

She sits with her head against the steering wheel. Moments later a chill runs up her spine and she is bathed in a sense of peace and calm. The weight is lifted from her chest and she resumes normal breathing. Awestruck, she does the only thing she can think of—she thanks whatever God is out there repeatedly, starts the engine and drives out of the cornfield and back down the highway to home, whatever that might be.

The divorce is not immediate. Their state requires a six month wait and counseling. The counselor says he can show them how to heal their relationship, but first they will have to heal themselves. She goes to work, and, although it is a see-saw process, she can feel herself grow. Gary struggles, too often it is easier to drown his pain in beer and whiskey then it is to hang it out on the line to dry in the fresh air. They finally agree to divorce. However, the cord connecting their hearts is only frayed, so, with the weight off, they begin to talk; they even decide to see each other.

Over the course of the next year she quits her job and moves out of state, a plan she put on the back burner when she met Gary. They continue to connect over the phone. He is coming to visit. They will just take things as they come. After picking him up at the airport she suggests a hike. The trail starts out steep and pretty much stays that way. Gary opens his water bottle, takes a swig and hands it to his wife—correction—his ex-wife. They walk in silence for the first quarter mile, conserving their limited oxygen supplies as their lungs stretch to meet the demand.

"You'll have to get your own place," she says, "and find a job."

"Yeah, I know," he replies after a moment.

She stares out at the earth as it slopes away to the valley.

"I have an application for a body shop here—I'm gonna send it in tomorrow," he continues.

"I thought you already filled one out and sent it in weeks ago. That's what you said in your letter."

"Oh, yeah, um, I misplaced it on the kitchen counter and I guess it never got in the mail," he stammers. "You know me, I'm not much on organization. I'm going to talk to the guy tomorrow."

The last word hangs in the air and takes on a life of its own. It grows long legs, spindly arms, a spineless skeleton with empty eye sockets in a vacant skull. It dances in front of her, a dance she recognizes from its many appearances during the ten years of their marriage. A thought slips in as she watches the dance: it's time to let this go. For once in her life she hates being right.

Gary feels the awkward silence building. God, he hates when she gets like this; it always makes him feel like groveling.

"Maybe you can help me look for a place," he stutters to hide his fears.

She stares at him but does not reply.

"When does your flight leave?" she asks after several minutes pass.

"Thursday around noon," Gary says puzzled. Hell, I just got here, he thinks. Her shoulders twitch at the thought of two more days. Why did she agree to keep seeing him and holding onto something that should have never been? They divorced six months ago and she even moved out of state. The feelings, it seems, take longer to die than the paperwork takes to clear the court and end up in a file cabinet somewhere.

How can she tell him? He is the one who walked out on her; she is the one who begged him to come back, who dragged him through session after session with the marriage counselor. Now, standing on top of the ridge looking down into Lost Man Lake, she knows with complete clarity that her life has a new path, very separate from his. Maybe it is the altitude that helped pick the lint from her eyes, maybe she finally knows herself well enough to not need someone, anyone, rather than the right one.

Gary leads the way back down the trail. They stop for a snack and marvel at the intricacies of the wild flowers: Indian paintbrushes, bluebells, mountain gentian and her favorite which does not have a name. It is a skinny purple petal with a small black ball hanging off the end on a thin black thread—they grow out of a six-inch stalk. As she stands up she catches a glimpse of Gary out of the corner of her eye, tan and handsome with a rugged muscular body. It's too bad, she thinks, it's just too bad.

"Where do you want to go to dinner?" Gary asks.

She thinks for a moment. "How about the Tattered Jeans? They have great burgers and I'm starved." She remembers her dishwashing days and smiles inwardly.

"Sounds good to me," Gary says as he unlocks the car and tosses in his pack. After dinner she uses exhaustion to head to bed early. Gary stays up to watch Jay Leno.

The next day Gary calls the body shop; the manager is on vacation, he says as he hangs up. "I'll just fill out the application and mail it. I can always call the guy and talk to him on the phone." A few hours later she checks her call log; the number to the body shop does not show up.

The car is hot and stuffy, even with the air conditioner on. Maggie parks the car in the close-in parking garage; this should not take long. Gary busies himself with his carry-on, zipping it up after putting his magazine away. He wants to freeze frame the moment, step out of the car and onto the plane, but her voice gets out before he has a chance. Through some kind of intermittent translator he catches words as they dodge his reason: "Time to let go... two different paths... it won't work..." She tries to use the new words with compassion, to somehow soften them, but she knows how they sound, just like the ones in the kitchen had sounded so many months ago. Gary wants to stick his fingers in his ears and scream to drown out the sound. What a bitch, he thinks. She begged me to come back just so she could dump me. It is just like her to have the last word. She never did give credit to anything I said or did.

He hears himself say "FINE!" watches his hand grab his bag and storms into the terminal. His angry backside is the last she ever sees of him.

31

topaz

You stared down death, you were stage 4b; I knew what that meant and tried not to say it: after surgery and radiation you wait; we walked and talked to chase away anxieties, troubled children and disintegrating marriages, we shared a communion of fear, hope, anger, respite and revival; I sat at your kitchen table asking why; you lay in your hospital bed asking why; neither required response except for a hand squeeze; we take so much from those whose lives bounce unexpectedly up against ours, I could write thank-you notes 24/7/365; sometimes someone's deep and unassuming strength humbles you to the point of tears and you stop, knowing that in that moment, life is both painful and exquisite and perfect; a hug, a word spoken at all diminishes the experience, so you sit silently admiring and thanking the gods for this blessing; from you I learned to be a friend, truly a friend.

THEY KEEP FISHING FOR THE VEIN, it keeps rolling. Twenty minutes later, they give up. Marilyn sits white-faced in the hematology lab while they go to get a butterfly set-up to go into the back of her hand. God, she hates having her blood drawn. A sweat breaks out on her forehead and upper lip. Her friend holds her other arm and rubs her back. You would think four children, two of whom are sampling life in ways she wishes they would not and one with serious health problems; a husband whose job is tenuous; and an invalid father would exempt her from the you-need-more-shit-in-your-life category, but it does not.

"Breast cancer! Shittin' breast cancer! Can you believe it? On top of everything else!"

Her friend just shakes her head. "I've come to the conclusion that there is no grand scheme of things, only random acts. I believe in the chaos theory that I heard proposed at a toxicology meeting I attended last year. The theory says that an event like cancer occurs when multiple random factors come together in a moment and trigger the waiting switch sitting in our DNA. Like we get a virus, are in a polluted environment, are under extreme stress, do not eat properly and have a mutant gene somewhere just waiting for all of these to come together at one time and whammo! Cancer."

Marilyn nods her head in agreement. All of her life certainly seems that way. Just a bunch of stuff that happens and the trick is to see how well you handle it.

Marilyn's friend continues, "Someone once told me that we keep being put in the same situation until we get it right." Her inner monologue runs on—damn, that means another marriage may be a possibility although I highly doubt it. Obviously, I still haven't got it right. Losing a husband to divorce is not the same as losing a part of her body although at times it feels like that.

After drawing blood, Marilyn is taken to the radiation lab and prepped. They draw lines with blue gentian ink to delineate the location where rads will enter the body in search of both errant and ordinary cells. Too bad for the ordinary ones, they go too; we are not at the point of selective therapy. It is a kill-them-all-and-hope-some-good-ones-grow-back methodology. It is like spraying Agent Orange on the jungles of Viet Nam to find Vietcong and oops if a few US soldiers happen to be in the line of fire. Her friend sits in the waiting room going over her pharmaceutical knowledge of the current therapies. Her expertise is in cardiovascular medications but she has some understanding of how cancer treatments work. Scientifically speaking, cancer treatment is still in the dark ages, just a step above leeches but even these rudimentary therapies are changing cancer from a death sentence to a life imprisonment term. After you get the all-clear there is always the chance of a recurrence. It's like a stalker: you keep checking over your shoulder to see if it's still there, never secure in knowing it has been eradicated.

They stop for ice cream on the way home. Marilyn feels exhausted; the treatments knock the stuffing out of her, along with the fact that there are still meals to cook, laundry to wash, dry, fold and put away, dishes to load and unload, and her father to check in on. Some days she thinks succumbing to the cancer is not a bad thing and feels immediately guilty. Her friend stays to help with laundry, dishes and dinner. Marilyn curls up in bed in sweats and an oversized t-shirt for a couple of hours, unable to fight the overwhelming load of life sitting on her chest. Sleep is an escape she greatly cherishes and does not understand why it would have negative psychological implications. She thinks all shrinks should take naps and learn to appreciate the healing power of sleep.

LESS THAN A YEAR LATER, Marilyn sits twisting and untwisting her purse strap until she hears her name called. Her feet move one in front of the other through the door and down the hallway into the office. Dr. Hamilton sits behind the big mahogany desk and peers over his pince-nez glasses.

"It's back" is the simple proclamation from his white-coatness. "We didn't get it all and we're going to have to go back in and another round of radiation will be needed following the surgery." The obligatory, "I'm sorry" follows.

Marilyn holds herself erect during her sentencing. She knows it's a stupid question but can't stop it from being asked inside her head: Why me? She dismisses it for all, its cliché. The real question is bigger. Why her and millions of others? There is more, there is always more: more bills, more work, more errands, more car breakdowns, heaters not working, demands on her time, sick children, asshole husbands. When would she run out of mores? Doesn't anyone ever reach enough? Can she just take a break from reality and float off to la-la land? She hears herself agree to the schedule of events like it is a summer camp agenda. In a fog, she rises and walks out of the office. On her way out the nurse hands her the paperwork, squeezing her hand in parting.

She makes the arrangements, all of them, just in case.

Marilyn makes plans to have a drink after work with her recently separated friend. It makes her feel better to know other people have shit in their lives, too. Not that she wishes it on them; she's just glad she's not alone. They head to the Green Iguana for chips, salsa and margaritas. Men are the main topic of conversation—the good ones, the bad ones and the ideal ones which do not exist. "I had one of our vendors come on to me last week" her friend reports. "Word must have gotten out that I'm separated and the buzzards are starting to circle. He's a squirrelly-looking guy, he's married and he smells bad. What the hell did he think I wanted with him?" Marilyn laughs. They trade jibes and stories for a couple of hours and then Marilyn drives her friend home. She invites her in for a nightcap. As the two women sip a final drink, the topic turns to her cancer.

"You haven't said a word all evening about your doctor's visit today. How did it go?" Maggie asks. Moments of silence pass, she glances over at Marilyn sitting on the couch and sees the answer in her face. They both empty their drinks and Marilyn heads home.

32

sepia

Damaged beyond repair, uncles are not supposed to force themselves on little girls, it was not your fault, your mother was wrong to disavow the events, all things led to wounds that will not close; from you I learned about a sadness so profound it needs its own country.

~~~

THE TWO WOMEN WALK ALONG A BEACH in Southern California, kicking at the sand to watch the turquoise droplets scatter in the moonlight. "Luminescence," says Tara, "that's what makes the waves and water drops glow in Southwest colors with each footfall." Her friend is fascinated and scuffs her toe with each step to watch the colors dance across the beach.

"I told my mother when I was sixteen. She told me I'd made it up, imagined it. Her brother would never do anything to hurt his niece, she said. Just put it out of your head, she said. It never happened. "For years I tried, but it still came out in my dreams— hairy grunting things holding me down. In college I went to a therapist and it helped some, at least she believed me and validated the injuries and the damage. But I still feel the shame and filth. At thirty-five I still think people see my sins and I feel a rusting in my womb. I don't know why Todd stays, I'm incapable of intimacy. It's an ugly world where a man can sit at the family table after molesting his ten-year-old niece." Her friend slips an arm around her shoulder, an invisible tremor registers and she steps back. There is no refuting that last statement so they walk back to the hotel to the sound of flip-flops slapping bare feet.

Back at her hotel room, Maggie wonders what to do with this knowledge. How can humans be so sick and cruel? Where is this God who supposedly looks out for children? She tries to reconcile this information with her logical brain but fails. Does evil really have to exist in order for us to know good? Some things you just have to put in the "it does not compute" part of your brain and leave it there for some future time. She puts her thoughts away for the night and crawls under the covers.

They meet for lunch the next day and act like the conversation never took place. Tara has recently moved to Southern California and her friend is in town for a business convention. They used to work together and have stayed friends. They make plans to shop and meet up with some mutual acquaintances for cocktails. As they make their way through the outdoor mall with its blooming flora and fresh air stalls, Tara talks about her new life. She and Todd are doing fine. His new position, which precipitated their move, is working out fine and he loves it. She is job hunting but not in any hurry. A little time off is nice. Setting up the new house has kept her busy. Her friend asks about their family plans. She knows this is a touchy subject but is curious. Tara is quiet for a while. "Todd would like to start one," is all she says and then busies herself with looking at a scarf.

Years later Tara gives in to Todd's pleading for a child. At her seven-month checkup Dr. Sorino stares at the screen and continues to move the wand across her protruding stomach. For what seems like hours she scans the screen. These moments take on a surrealist quality. She hears herself say the words "no heartbeat"... "I'm sorry". Tara's small shoulders drop, imperceptibly, she stares blankly out the window. Todd keeps asking if she is sure and when the realization sinks in he collapses into sobbing. It is a girl; they name her Sarah and lay her to rest next to her grandmother. Two years later Amanda arrives. Todd is ecstatic; Tara goes through the motions.

Interlude XV

"...The officiate enjoins all to listen to the beautiful words of John Denver's For You."

> *Just to look in your eyes again*
> *Just to lay in your arms*
> *Just to be the first one always there for you*
> *Just to live in your laughter*
> *Just to sing in your heart*
> *Just to be every one of your dreams come true*
>
> *Just to sit by your window*
> *Just to touch in the night*
> *Just to offer a prayer each day for you*
> *Just to long for your kisses*
> *Just to dream of your sighs*
> *Just to know that I'd give my life for you*
>
> *For you for the rest of my life*
> *For you all the best of my life*
> *For you alone, only for you...*

33

yellow

You gave us all a lesson in unconditional love; from you I learned how to give without speaking and how to die with dignity.

CHLOE'S BLOND HAIR GLISTENS IN THE SUNLIGHT. She stretches and relaxes — another day of being attentive to those around her. Chloe heads upstairs to the bedrooms. She gently nudges her young girl, letting her know it is time for school. Next she wakes the masters of the house. They both have jobs to get off to while she keeps the house in order. Her favorite part of the day is the time spent while running with the mistress of the house. She shares her day and tales of the corporate world's crazies with Chloe while they jog past rows of corn and tranquil pastoral scenes. Wonderful scents abound, and not so wonderful ones as they pass the pig farms.

The owners are nice and allow her a lot of freedom. Her chores are minimal. She has free meals and a place to sleep each night. Not a bad deal. She has served this family for twelve years now. It has changed, its master and girl have left, one due to divorce and the other to college. Her mistress continues to need her services and Chloe enjoys the job. Although the mistress still jogs, she has had to curtail the activity due to joint problems. Truth be told, the mistress probably is not far behind in that category. They have both slowed down over the years. They have new surroundings now too; large red cliffs frame the backyard replacing green hillsides. She likes the change; it suits her bones better. She wishes it were just her bones; she has been feeling very run down lately and finding it difficult to breathe. Should I tell the mistress, she wonders?

One night as they watch TV together, Chloe slumps over and cannot move. She is rushed to the clinic; weeks later the diagnosis is hemangiosarcoma, a cancer of the blood vessels. Sadly, there is not much they can do except keep her comfortable. Her mistress dotes on her. Chloe sees the tears she tries to hide while brushing her hair. She strokes Chloe's head gently with the brush and brings her favorite foods. Chloe wishes she could eat them but nothing sits right most days. Occasionally, her youthful spunk returns and they enjoy a day of levity and false hope. The young girl of the house is now a young woman. She comes to visit Chloe most weekends, a sad commingling of happy memories and prescience of the future. They laugh about the time Chloe, running full speed down a hill, was unable to stop and sent the young girl crashing head over heels into the tall grass, and the both of them rolling around in the aftermath.

Chloe senses her final days and is at peace. She does what she can to thank the family that has sheltered her for a lifetime and loved her as a member. When she can no longer climb the stairs they bring a bed down to the kitchen for her and lie for hours telling stories of their lives together. She curls up in their warmth and her breathing comes easier.

Finally, the day comes when they have to say good-bye to their dear friend. The sadness overwhelms them. The veterinarian arrives in the morning and gives them a few moments alone before slipping the needle from his bag. Maggie and Grace hold each other and sob as the vet lets himself out the door. The emptiness is like a black hole that swallows them and no amount of light can reach them. Pictures outline the passage of the years: Chloe and the ten year old Grace; at Grace's sixteenth birthday and then high school graduation. Anniversaries, birthdays, holidays; there they are together, smiling, happy. On the wall the pictures stop. Who will ever love them as unconditionally, day after day, asking so little and giving so much?

34

translucent

You held a mirror to my face and had the courage to show me how I looked to the rest of the world, I never knew you well, but you gave me an incredible gift for my fortieth birthday, it was small and thin and contained everything I was searching for in my life; it had humor, guidance, wisdom, and tools for change; it was a new way to look at the world, one which rang so true it made me anxious to not do what I had spent a lifetime doing; from your gift I found the truth and was both humbled by and hysterical about its simplicity; from you I learned that being right was not as important as being human.

ALLYSIA GLANCES UP AT THE POSTER of "Aanold" on the back of her door and then at the clock. Another two hours to go and she is already brain dead. The protocol review meeting is tomorrow and she has to nail down all the details before the Ph.D.s get hold of it. If she leaves it up to them, it will be the most convoluted, complicated, confused and useless clinical trial ever conducted. They can take a simple double-blind trial and turn it into a Frankenstein, complete with neck bolts. She rubs her eyes and tries again to focus on the swimming black forms on the page. The phone rings and for once she welcomes the diversion. Her boss wants a word with her. "Okay, I'll be right over," she replies.

Outside of work they have become relatively close but at work they keep it all business. Her boss has mentored her into the business and she is mostly grateful for the guidance. Allysia takes a seat opposite the boss and asks, "What's up?"

"Dr. Brooks wants to shift gears again on the hypertension study. He thinks we need to include patients with renal impairment instead of keeping the population homogenous. I tried to dissuade him, but to no avail. Any suggestions?"

Allysia thinks for a moment. "Does he realize the number of side effects will skyrocket and it's going to end up in the labeling?"

"I've tried that tack. He's convinced the drug is so clean it won't matter," her boss replies.

"It's not the drug, it's the disease that's going to jack up the reported side effects," Allysia offers.

"I scheduled a meeting for tomorrow at one o'clock. Can you come back me up?"

"Sure, I'll be done with my protocol review meeting in the morning, and pending any major disasters, I should be able to attend."

"Thanks, I appreciate the support. Hey, what's up with Nora? I've been waiting for reports from her for weeks now and haven't seen a one. Do you know her very well?"

Allysia considers her response; she can not say she knows her. Nora is friendly with the people on her project but does not socialize outside that group. The few conversations she has been privy to seem to be company and boss bashing so Allysia did not join in. The company is going through tough times and the D word, downsizing, is being whispered. The overall atmosphere is pretty depressing if you think about it, but Allysia chooses to focus on her work instead. Somehow, life has a way of working out if you just let it. She is willing to trust the fates. Change is inevitable in the pharmaceutical world and work generally plentiful, so she is not overly concerned. She had once worked for three companies and never left her desk. The hostile takeover, buyout and merger game is alive and well in this industry. She does not envy her boss.

If the rumors are true, she will be the person deciding who stays and who goes in their group.

"I really don't know her very well, but I will say she has a negative impact on those close to her," is Allysia's measured reply. Her boss thanks her for her input and Allysia returns to her office

Her boss picks up the memo she had covered up on her desk when Allysia came in. She is going to have to halve her workforce. She did not sleep last night, weighted down with the responsibility. Does she give people fair warning that they are on the list or just let the axe fall? It will be two weeks before they announce the layoffs. She opts for giving clues so that people can start job hunting before the crowd hits the streets. She will let Allysia's group know they are safe and start warning others about the pending changes.

The rumor mill works like a wildfire with Santa Ana winds. Relief and anger mix in the hallways and behind closed doors.

Allysia is grateful for the news but feels bad for those whose lives are about to be up-ended. She is not so sure her boss should have forewarned people. Maybe the swift swipe of the sword would have been kinder. Morale is at an all-time low. When the day comes it is like a series of funerals, everyone saying good-bye. Half the group is packing up their offices, the other half hiding in theirs. The best of the group being let go already have some interviews set up. The rest will receive employment counseling and any training they need.

Later that day it is announced that her boss is being promoted and will be heading up the entire department instead of just certain projects. It is not that she does not deserve it, but it is bad timing and is going to cause more internal combustion. It is not good to appear to profit from other people's adversity, Allysia thinks.

Her boss is a perfectionist, driven to achieve, and expects high standards and output from all, not bad traits when mixed with a dose of compassion but her boss lives for her job and forgets people have lives outside the building. She has already heard the grumbling in the halls about working for "Miss Perfect."

The corporate rule is that all layoffs, firings, etc. take place on

Friday, that way people have a chance to cool down before they come back to work. That night Allysia and the boss meet for a drink. Her boss looks drained and is not in a celebratory mood.

"It's awful," she says after taking a long sip of her wine. I had no idea how bad this would be. How in the hell do I get people to focus on work with the grim reaper hiding in every corner? I know they won't think this is the end of the cuts..."

Allysia sits, quietly listening, but her first thought is "Just be human. Let people adjust and don't demand too much right away."

"...These projects have to stay on schedule if the rest of the company is to survive. I'm over the shock of the pending divorce and find work to be better than Xanax. Pouring myself into work is the best distraction for me. I don't understand why people want to dwell on this stuff. It won't change anything."

Her boss stops and looks up at Allysia. "What are you thinking?"

Maybe it is the wine or maybe the events of the day but Allysia decides to go for it. "I think you need to be human and allow people some time to adjust. Not everyone is like you; they don't keep their feelings under tight control. These are their friends that were let go, they feel sad for them and guilty because they get to stay. Just give them some time. In the big scheme of things, the future of this company is not what matters to them; it's their friends and families. Not everyone wants to climb the corporate ladder." Allysia takes a deep breath and waits.

After a long pause her boss asks, "Is that what people think of me?"

"Well, yes."

"So I'm the Ice Woman I hear comments about in the restroom. Ouch." Another long pause as she drains her glass. "I guess I do push pretty hard and get too focused. It's hard being a woman in a man's world. I adopted male behavior in order to survive and never questioned whether it was good or not. It's just how it was. I was trained not to show feelings at work; to detach and be objective. I think I do it well by the sounds of it," she says through the hurt. They order another round.

On the way home, a litany of rationalizations and excuses run through her boss's head. They scroll across her mental screen like the dancing elephants in *Fantasia*. This is work, not a social event; people need direction and to stay on task; she is helping them to develop, showing them the ropes; doesn't she always bring donuts on Fridays and encourage birthday celebrations? But in the end she agrees, she is just too, too, too intense, serious, and oblivious to normal human interaction. She has learned to shut out a lot of things. Her thoughts go back to the days after Gary walked out. God, I was a basket case, hiding in my office, crying until five o'clock. and then going home. No one hounded me for documents sitting on my desk. They quietly took them and finished them for me and never said a word.

NEXT FRIDAY will be her boss's Big Four-O, so Allysia racks her brain for an idea: coffee cup, business card holder, pen. No, she wants something different. Her boss is worth more than the usual office gifts. Allysia likes her, she works hard and works everyone hard, but she's fair. At parties her boss entertains with a sarcastic sense of humor and leaves her suit at the office. She knows down deep that this woman has a lot of feelings and is caring. Maybe she just needs a way to bring them to the surface.

As she wanders through the mall she's stumped. She thinks, jewelry, no, too hard to pick for someone else; music, same thing. Candles are a bit overdone nowadays. Her feet stop in front of a Covers and Spines Bookstore. That's it, a book. Okay, but which one of the thousands will she like? Allysia thumbs through the new bestsellers—nothing catches her eye. She browses the travel section, knowing her friend does a fair amount. On to the cookbooks, but too overwhelmed by the choices, she moves on to photography, poetry, philosophy—she stops. There at eye level is a tiny treatise called *Tao Te Ching*, translation by Stephen Mitchell. It's Allysia's bible, but will her colleague like it? Reviewing her mental log of her boss's personality she decides to take a chance. Over a few too many beers they had shared a need for spirituality in their lives but both denounced organized religion. This will be perfect.

Friday after work, the Hawthorne Pharmaceuticals gang descends on Flatliners Bar for birthday festivities: a big Four-O with lots of black balloons. Drinks are ordered and gifts pile up. The after work suits are grazing on the happy hour appetizers. The guest of honor bandies jokes and accepts her role of sacrificial lamb for the evening. Geritol, hair dye, thick glasses, Metamucil, Depends and various other trappings of age are offered up as gifts. She takes it all in stride and gives back whenever possible. At the bottom of the pile is a small, thin package. She opens it. It is a book entitled *Tao te Ching*.

"It's a favorite of mine," Allysia chimes in, "and I hope you'll like it." Her boss thanks her and the festivities continue.

The next day Maggie slips the book from her bag of gifts and opens it randomly and reads:

> *In dwelling, live close to the ground.*
> *In thinking, keep to the simple.*
> *In conflict, be fair and generous.*
> *In governing, don't try to control.*
> *In work, do what you enjoy.*
> *In family, be completely present.*
>
> *When you are content to be simply yourself*
> *and don't compare or compete,*
> *everybody will respect you.*
>
> *...Nothing in the world*
> *is as soft and yielding as water.*
> *Yet for dissolving the hard and inflexible*
> *nothing can surpass it.*
>
> *The soft overcomes the hard;*
> *the gentle overcomes the rigid.*

> *Everyone knows this is true,*
> *but few can put it into practice.*

She resolves to learn to put it into practice.

Once again a book appears in her life, one that causes an imperceptible change on the outside and a profound change on the inside. She reads it again and again marveling at its truth and simplicity. This is it. The Way it is called and she knows instinctively what it means even if she can not put it into words. Now if she can just embody it. Her Tai Chi classes have started her on a new path and certainly this book has come into her possession deliberately. She determines to stop making things happen and learn to let them happen. Her western brain struggles with the concepts but the heart in the center she understands.

Monday, she shows up in linen slacks and a pale pink blouse, no severe suit. She stops in the break room to chat with colleagues over a cup of coffee. Next she pops her head into each cube and office and greets each person. This feels good, she thinks as she makes her way down the hall. She stays to catch up on their children's latest accomplishments or shenanigans with those who extend the invitation. Back in her office she sends out a memo announcing a department breakfast on Friday at a local restaurant. It will start at nine o'clock and no one is to come in any earlier. There will be no agenda or action items aside from good food and conversation. How freeing all this feels. She picks up the phone and dials the florist. When Allysia gets home that night she is greeted by a beautiful floral arrangement.

Interlude XVI

~~

"...Maggie takes the paper from the officiate, hands shaking, clears her throat and begins."

David, My Sweet, David:
    I remember sitting on the living room floor back in December four years ago. You had brought over a white board and magnets to show me how to read the river. I watched as you drew the river course and placed magnets here and there to represent rocks. Your voice said, "As you approach a bend the water flows fastest against the wall." But the voice in my head was speaking much louder and it said "He's the one..."
    A canyon wren's call punctuates the silence, the audience waits for her to resume.
    Maggie takes a deep breath, breathing in strength and calm as she stares into his moistened eyes...
    "...He's the one. He's the one you've searched for all your life." My next thought was to be soft, kind and compassionate and welcome you into my life. Today, I stand next to you, humbled by the blessings you have brought (Maggie's

voice quivers) and ever mindful of the immense responsibility to protect and cherish these gifts. I am yours, mind, body and soul until the canyon wren runs out of song.

I love you.

35

poppy

Wild woman supreme, red hair flying down the road in your Porsche—our single nights punctuated with drinking, dancing and guy hustling—pickens were few so we headed home laughing; we shared our wounds that we hid under lace blouses and tight blue jeans; people we trusted betrayed us, ones we loved denied us, we sought answers fruitlessly until no answer became necessary; because of you, I found family a long way from home.

―※―

VANESSA LACES UP HER ROLLER BLADES while her friend pulls water bottles from the car. Both of them take wobbly first steps. She bends over to wipe the dust from her skates. With each stroke their legs firm up and soon they are gliding over the path. "It's only been a month," Vanessa says. "I miss her and hate her all at the same time. Does that make sense? She wasn't a happy person but she was my mom. Some days I still sense her in the house, she's mad about something and I'm cringing. I wish I could have understood her better or maybe I wish she understood herself better."

They approach the first downhill section and grind hard on the brakes. "Whoa," Vanessa yells as she careens out of control down the slight embankment and around a bend. Her friend follows with flailing arms and just barely manages to stay upright. They both puff up the next hill.

"I'm out of shape," Van grunts.

"Me too," is the reply from her lagging friend.

"Remind me again why we're doing this—oh yeah, some crap about being healthy."

Her friend just laughs.

"So, anyhow, now I guess I go forward and try to figure myself out. I know some of my depressive tendencies come from my mom, but I'm clueless as to what to do about them. What should I do?"

"I don't know," replies her friend. "I caught the same disease from my mother. It took several therapists and some positive changes and eventually, I outgrew it, like the ugly dress you get from an aged aunt for Christmas."

They cruise along a flat section. The river runs along their left side and they watch as ducks circle in the inlets. The sun beats down but the trees overhanging the trail keep them cooled. They stop to rest on a bench at the turnaround and realize they have forgotten their water bottles. Vanessa reads the sign tacked up to the post opposite the bench.

> Beware; a mountain lion has recently been sighted along this trail. Do not leave small children or pets unattended!

An uneasy feeling like being watched makes Vanessa turn in her seat and survey the area. Her friend does the same, straining her eyes to see into the brush. "Hey, let's not hang out here like bait," says Van.

"Fine with me."

On their way back to the car, Vanessa resumes her reverie about her mother. "In some ways she spoiled me and in others she abandoned me. Physically, I got my way but emotionally she was so distant that I felt adrift. Sometimes her sadness just overwhelmed me and I had to get away. I remember a time when she was sitting in the living room, just staring and when I asked her what was wrong, she said, 'You. You were wrong, I shouldn't have brought you into this world'. I just stood there, stunned. You know me;

usually anyone who gives me shit's in for it. But there was just nothing I could say. I walked out the door, hopped in my car and didn't come home for a week. When I did it was as though nothing had happened.

"We never talked about anything. We had planted all these landmines and then just walked around them like pieces of furniture. Soon they just crowded me out of the house. I struck out to make my own life. I found a town hundreds of miles away and got a job at a travel agency. Next came a series of poor choices in men and finally a child. The father never wanted anything to do with Sasha or me, so we just got by on our own."

Back at home, her friend contemplates Van's last statement. She has been getting by on her own for a lifetime. As a child she figured out the only person she could count on was herself, and, time and again, life came around to prove her right.

She picks up the phone to call her sister, her lifeline. Since she and Jackie can no longer meet after work or spend Saturdays shopping, the phone connection has to substitute. Living over a thousand miles from her family both saddens and gladdens her. Too much family causes annoyance, too little leaves lonely in its wake. Her daughter resides four hours away, too far for a day's visit. Weekends have to be cleared to accommodate the distance. She wishes they could have Sunday dinners together and play Trivial Pursuit in the evenings. Grace has grown from an unbendable oak into a flexible willow during her young adulthood and expresses wisdom beyond her years. How she wishes she could pop in for a cup of coffee and chat about the day's events. But, once again, the cold airwaves must suffice.

Van's reminiscing about her mother inflames ashes she thought she doused long ago. Memories of her mother filter through an opaque haze, like being privy to someone else's dreams. It has been over twenty years since her mother swallowed a bottle of pills and chased it with a fifth of booze. What frightens her is those moments like yesterday where she hears her voice echoing back from the canyon walls and mistakes it for her mother's or a glance in the mirror reveals a face and body like the one that repelled her all those years ago. The anger which once consumed her has been softened by the winds of time and has taken on the shape of the desert rocks of the San Rafael Swell where she camps in the springtime. Her jagged edges have been worn away. Those litanies of her mother's faults have been carried off by those same winds. She knows Vanessa will also journey through the canyons and become molded by the elements within and without.

A few days later, Vanessa walks next door to her friend's house and invites her to dinner. They chat out in the garden where she is cursing the weeds.

"What can I bring?"

"How about a bottle of wine?" Van suggests. "I have some steaks to throw on the grill and a salad. We'll keep it simple. The whole family will be there so be prepared."

"I love your family," Maggie says as she pulls on a deep-rooted weed.

"Yeah, that's because they're not YOUR family."

"I suppose you're right, but being thousands of miles from mine makes it nice to be a part of yours."

36

purple

School is not your thing, work is not your thing, sweetness is and maybe it will be enough to get you through life; we hiked in the snow, skied, learned to snowboard, laughed and cried; from you I learned patience, the Tao, long-term commitment and perseverance.

THE BIG BROTHER/BIG SISTER RECREATION CENTER is teeming with over-energized adolescents. Paika stands just inside the door surveying the throng hoping to see a familiar face. A short woman with brown hair comes up and asks her to play ping-pong.

"I don't know how," she replies.

"That's okay, I'm pretty crummy myself," the woman responds as she picks up a paddle and ball.

Paika ponders the request a moment longer and then says, "Sure."

The lady drops the ball and taps it over the net. Paika swings too hard and the ball flies across the room. "Oops."

"What's your name?" the lady asks as she retrieves the ball from beneath a table.

"My name is Paika."

"Okay, Paika, where do you go to school?"

"I go to James Taft Elementary."

"What grade are you in?"

"Fifth grade," she grunts as she retrieves the ball from under a couch.

The ball continues to spend more time on the floor than on the table. Soon it is eight o'clock and the recreation center is closing. Paika says good-bye and heads out to the parking lot to meet her mom.

Weeks later, Paika and her mom sit in the caseworker's office, forms in hand. She is getting a Big Sister. There is a knock on the door, the caseworker opens it and there stands the ping-pong lady.

"Hi Paika," she says as she enters the office.

"Hi, whatchadoinghere?"

"I'm going to be a Big Sister."

"I see you two have met," interjects the caseworker

"Yep, we played ping-pong at the recreation center a couple of weeks ago."

"Well, good, it gives us a place to start."

At the conclusion of the interview, they agree to give it a go.

Paika jumps up and down on the way to the car, "I have a Big Sister." She hopes it will be fun. They make a date to go to a movie. Over the next several years they roller blade, ride bikes, eat pizza, play ping-pong and hike. Hiking is their favorite so they are excited as they plan their first overnight camping and hiking trip. It's been three years since they first played ping-pong and Paika has grown four inches. She is as tall as her Big Sister now.

The day is sunny as they head up the trail but soon the clouds roll in and the sky opens up. Their ponchos slap against their blue thighs. Snow stings their eyes as they slip over snow banks. Their socks stick to their frozen toes. Her Big Sister starts up a song to distract them from their misery.

> Old McDonald had a farm, EIEIO, and on this farm he had some jerks, EIEIO, with a jerk, jerk here and a jerk, jerk there, here a jerk, there a jerk everywhere a jerk, jerk, Old McDonald had a farm EIEIO.

They laugh as they make up their own lyrics. Paika's boyfriend has just broken up with her so she dedicates the jerk verse to him.

It was sunny when they set out that morning so shorts and tennis shoes seemed like a good idea. Now a thought enters Paika's mind: Why didn't her Big Sister forewarn her about afternoons in the mountains? After all she used to live up here. Her feet are dry; she is wearing hiking boots. Nice job taking care of the kid.

Her Big Sister or Big as they call them, starts up a new song and Paika joins in—it's a nasty little ditty and they laugh as they sing.

> "Do your tits hang low can you swing them to and fro, can you tie them in a knot, can you tie them in a bow, can you throw them over your shoulder like a continental soldier, do your tits hang low."

This is Paika's Big Sister's rendition of an old classic where she has substituted tits for ears. Paika is fourteen and she loves it. They sing it several times over as they slog over the soggy trail. Aspen Creek Falls is their destination and they are not to be deterred. They finally arrive at the falls, have someone snap their picture and practically run the three and a half miles back to the car. Big starts the engine and blasts the heater.

"Damn, I'm frozen," she says.

"Yeah, well, you didn't have tennis shoes on. I can hardly feel my feet."

Their thighs are red raw from the snow, wind and plastic ponchos slapping them. They change into dry clothes in the bathroom of the Tattered Jeans and wolf down cheeseburgers and hot chocolate until their color returns to normal.

Back at the pop-up trailer in the campground, they play cards and joke about the day. Seven miles of hiking does them in and they snuggle into their sleeping bags by nine o'clock. Sometime during the night Paika awakes to icy fingers on her face and arms. She thinks she is dreaming and she's back on the trail. Her eyes adjust and she remembers that she is camping and, once again, cold has crawled under her skin. She rubs her arms, hoping to bring back warmth. Soon she is shivering all over. She hears Big tossing and turning, then "Damn it's cold!" What the hell happened to the heater?" Paika laughs in spite of the ache in her bones. Big climbs out of her sleeping bag to check the heater. "Crap, it's out", she hears her mumble. "God, I hate being cold. Where are the matches? Ouch, dammit."

Paika hears her foot come in contact with the table leg and laughs. Big does not think it's funny. After one hundred failed attempts to light the heater, she gives up and they gather all the blankets and sleeping bags onto one bed and crawl in together. Finally they are somewhere near normal body temperature and fall asleep.

As the sun climbs down the cliff side, they stretch stiff limbs. The hike and cold has turned their muscles into something that feels like silly putty left in the freezer. Paika looks over at Big; her hair is sticking out in ten directions. Paika laughs as she tries to tame it with her hands.

"Well, you don't look like Miss America yourself," Big says with wounded pride. Finally, they pry themselves out from their cocoon and make some breakfast. Soon they pack up and hit the road to home. Paika can not wait to do it again but next time they have to go somewhere warm.

It's the fall and Paika is now in high school. Big helps with homework; well, she tries to anyway.

"What do you mean you didn't turn it in? We spent four hours last week getting you caught up on assignments." Big stares at Paika, incredulously.

"I don't know, I just lost it or something," she mumbles.

"But I even gave you a folder for each subject and a place to put each assignment until you turned it in. How could you have lost it?" Big is befuddled. Not only is Paika absent repeatedly but even when she is in school she rarely does the work. She is a bright girl and her yearly testing shows her at or above her grade level, but she is barely passing any of her classes. Big talks to her mom who is clueless to explain Paika's behavior.

It's frustrating; they have been Big/Little Sisters over four years and Paika's school pattern is unchanged. Big thought she was going to make an instant change in this girl and wonders at the notion of continuing. Maybe she isn't any good at influencing this girl; maybe she needs someone who is stronger or one who has a grasp of child psychology. She has tried everything: cajoling, demanding, enticing, bribing, rewarding, denying, but nothing seems to work. She bought her a ski pass which could be used when she proved her work was done. Paika loves snowboarding above all else, but even that did not get her to complete her school assignments and turn them in. Big throws up her hands and stays away for a while.

During the weeks in hiding Big spends time searching and analyzing her technique, approach, and, finally, her heart. She remembers back to her own troubled start and how she was almost thirty years old before she got her life on track. There were people who had tried to help her. Irene reached out to her in high school and Rosie patiently taught her to knit, sew and tell the truth. It must have hurt them to watch as she went down wrong path after wrong path. Maggie picks up the phone and dials Paika's number.

"Hello, is Paika there?"

They make plans to go see the movie *Titanic*.

37

crystal

Your bird by bird is my bible; it sits next to me like a best friend and encourages me, I put pen to paper and fill one-inch picture frames; I laughed till I cried while reading Operating Instructions; *I have decided to give all of my characters little tiny penises, male and female alike, to ward off any libel; from you I learned how to quiet my inner critic and let the story tell itself and when the muse takes lunch, I re-read and edit.*

―∞―

ANNE SITS IN FRONT OF ANOTHER GROUP of author wannabes. She reads their faces: hope, insecurity, fear, determination. She plans to use each forlorn and anticipatory look to create a masterpiece of humor. Their eyes plead to be recognized, singled out as brilliant. Anne worries about whether or not she unplugged the toaster. She once read it was the number one cause of house fires. She brings her attention back to the group in front of her. There is a blue-eyed woman in the second row. Her pen furiously making curly-cue letters strung together to create redeemable forms. Anne notes that the time is up and each in turn reads their palms for the class. They tell stories of unions made and lost; life spans, long and short; and happiness or the lack thereof. Their characters are short, tall, fat, skinny, bald, tan, pale, blond, dark, curious, boring, handsome, arrogant, LIFELESS! She tells them to take their characters to lunch and get to know them. Interview them, she says, as potential mates, nanny's or best friends. What's there favorite color? Do they slurp their coffee and pick their noses? Do they own forty-seven pairs of shoes but wear only one ugly black pair outside the house? Look under their fingernails—what kind of dirt do you find?

They come back after lunch and have given CPR to their kooks and confidants. The next round of readings revives Anne. The woman with blue eyes gives her protagonist perfectly coiffed hair and a drawer full of socks arranged by color and activity. Shirts and pants hang similarly in the closet, but his Old English sheep dog sleeps on his bed. It is covered with dog hair. She likes the contrast of order overshadowed by chaos. She might just make it, Anne thinks.

Back at home, after the workshop, Maggie opens the box of business cards, the ones with the B.S., M.S. after her name, and dumps them into the trashcan. She hits the speed dial and talks into the headset inches from her chin.

"It's time to make a change," she says. "No, I will not reconsider. It's been great but it's time to follow a new path. Thanks, I'll miss you too." She hangs up. It is time to ask that question Sydney asked so many years ago again.

Her next call is to Sydney to tell her the good news. "I'm done, no more. It's time to follow my dream, one that is both old and new. I'm going to be a writer. I finally have the courage and requisite skills to make a go of it."

"Wow, that's fantastic," is Sydney's astonished reply.

"It's your fault again," her friend announces. "If you hadn't taken the two years off to paint, throw pots, garden, do stained glass, golf and ski, I wouldn't have been envious and gone looking for a way to do the same."

"Hey, let's get together for a night of celebration and debauchery," Sydney suggests.

"Fine with me. What works for you?"

"How about next weekend?" Sydney offers.

"Let's do it! I'll roll in around five-ish on Friday, so get the martini shaker chillin'."

38

cayenne

I read Red *and marveled at its roots in earth, its ties to all things living; it tied me to my earth and awakened my muse, Pan played and the words flowed, I received inspiration and dusted off the need to put pen to paper, I took* Refuge *in your willingness to expose your tender belly to the world.*

TERRY TEMPEST WILLIAMS WALKS AMONG THE RED ROCKS, touching them to feel their pulse. Her heels are roughened from open sandals and bareness. The bareness beckons the rocks and she unstraps the worn sandals. The sand is scorching but the calluses serve her well. She wishes for those calluses around her heart sometimes. A fat lizard scurries across the path just in front of her toes. The blue of the sky burns her eyes. Conversations from last night's environmental meeting play like a marquee banner in her head. Who wins her allegiance? She feels like a rope in a tug of war—family, finance, beliefs clash with intuition, life forms and friends.

A hopeful author tries to know Terry through the lines she writes, and, more importantly, what comes between the lines. Maggie drove through Castle Valley one Sunday, hoping to get a glimpse of Terry. Faulty thinking rolled down lanes of paving; maybe by riding the same highway she will pick up the thread Terry unraveled on the side of the road and it will weave a tapestry of words worthy of the eyes of others.

In an attempt to connect with your *Red* energy she dedicates a poem to you:

> her gift fills me like
> good wine
> warm flesh
> womaness
> aching to gather
> red earth,
> ancient art,
> sand after rain,
> soft kisses,
> whispering flute in
> camplight,
> generations
> of risk and
> ruin, pain
> inflicted, wounds bound
> and threads
> tying all
> animate, inanimate,
> spiritual to all
> animate, inanimate,
> spiritual, to all...

Interlude XVII

～

David takes Maggie's hand and looks into her eyes.

"What I want to say to you today...

I am giving you my heart and soul for safe-keeping" (tears well up and Maggie reaches up to his cheek to brush them away)

David tries again...

"I am giving you my heart and soul for safe keeping for I know that you will guard them with care.

Know that I love only you and that I will cherish and honor each promise and vow.

Together, we will find new canyons to hike and taller mountains to climb

I promise... (his eyes run down his face, his chest heaves with the effort of holding on, Maggie gently says "It's okay," and squeezes his hand, "take your time").

"I am so sorry," David says barely audible.

Maggie repeats, "It's okay."

Somewhat composed, David continues...

I promise you that I will take special care of you and Grace. I will continue to find ways to surprise, entertain and delight you. I am humbled, honored, proud, and thrilled to be with you now and forever.

As I have promised you and Grace, I will never leave either of you.

We are truly blessed, you and I, for God has been exceedingly kind and generous. With special prayers of thanks and respect, we are now a-sail on our journey.

Good friends and family have been at our side as we have grown our love from chance meetings to today's commitment. With their love and support we will toast them each year, forever.

You are my love... and my life, Maggie

I love you so...

The sunlight glistens off David's face. Maggie hands him the tissue she has hidden in her bouquet.

39

moenkopi

The yin to my yang; "you don't make sense, I don't make sense, together we make sense"—it is a line from the movie with christian slater and marissa tomei called Untamed Heart; I see you with tubes coming out of your neck—it scares me, I gather my frayed nerves and stand with sword ready to defend you against mortality; it's too soon, I say, and he retreats; in exchange you give me courage to follow my dreams and make me believe I can; I marvel at your artistry of vision, life, breath, I know I am finally home, at home, a home.

―∽―

DAVID SITS WITH PEN POISED, wondering how to express love at sixty-some years old. What a time to have found it. He is befuddled at its appearance this late in life. He was pretty well resigned to a life alone; maybe he would get a dog, but, a girlfriend? That just did not seem even remotely plausible.

He invites his girlfriend; the word feels strange on this tongue, to join him in Chaco Canyon, to honor the ancients, drink wine to the spirits and commune with nature. She accepts his written invitation. He starts his response:

> My Colorado Sweetie:
> A champagne bubbly, Mimosa scintillating, Bloody Mary zipping, Luna de Luna calming, Margarita exhilarating,

Tuaca soothing days wishes to you this day. I hope today finds you with a warm breeze in your hair, a song on your lips and a poem in your heart...

As I begin the planning process for Chaco, I am reminded that no one has cared to make the trek to the canyon with me... I will pay homage to the Fates and say... destiny has drawn us near. When I called you back this morning, I said that I was glad to meet you. That would have to be the understatement of the century. Glad pales a distant last. Exuberant and privileged gets closer. Everywhere I go now I focus on the things and vistas around me; the beauty, the textures, the wonder...

I again read your letter... Chaco Canyon in the spring, river reading lessons, and some joy in reading my errant letters. The warm images painted, the flowing passion cascading, races with wonder and genuine torrents of newly discovered emotions, my allowance spent, or so I thought, my purse is again filled.

Letters pour from him daily. Some he mails, some he drives in the wee hours of the morning to hand deliver to her mailbox. He sits in his truck staring at her bedroom in the southwest corner of the house where he knows she is sleeping, barely breathing. He puts his hand to her chest sometimes, just to make sure she has not joined the spirit world. He tucks notes into her briefcase and suitcase as another business trip takes her from his sight. They are like crumbs to help her find her way back home. Bear sits on his computer those days as a solace. She gave him Bear, a soft curly teddy bear, to hold on to nights she inhabits the Marriott Hotels of the East Coast on business. She cries at the discovery of his words falling out of folded clothes.

On Valentine's Day he sends her a letter of thanks, thanks for:

    — trading bantered passages at Capitol Reef

    — snuggling in the tent

    — watching the raspberry Borealis

— tracing your hand across my back as you pass
— taking him to the hospital during his heart attack
— loving him outside the box

David stops himself at page five.

He thinks back to the days when he hid out in the Canyonlands area of Utah because he needed a place big enough to hold his pain. His wife, correction, ex-wife, moved to Idaho with his only son. The picture of Dan's little face staring out the back window of the car, a pudgy little hand waving, ripped his heart out of his chest. The pain was a mixture of heartache at seeing his child disappear, regret for not doing more to save his marriage, and disappointment in himself. He was not the father and husband he should have been. His selfishness put the little boy in the back seat and sent him down the road. How many nights did he need to drink beer and bullshit with the boys? The sensations overwhelmed him and he ran and hid in one of the most achingly beautiful places on this earth.

After years of running the small store outside the Canyonland National Park boundaries, he returned to Colorado and his previous life. A couple more unsuccessful liaisons and business deals later he hung it up. He was nearing sixty and tired of fighting. He had tried for years to make a living in an economically depressed area of Colorado. He had tried to find love and a family, to no avail. He let his only son drift away fearing he had nothing to give him. His spirit had flown, and all he had left was his empty shell. His family had property south of Tucson, maybe he would hide out there this time.

He went to Tucson to die; when that was not forthcoming, he returned to Colorado and life. He met her in limbo; his heart still in the cryogenics lab. She is younger, a friend of an old neighbor. Her youth is contagious and he finds himself daring to dream again. He is greedy and wants more years. He wishes he could reclaim the ones he wasted. But his focus is forward now, not back.

Like every couple they have a unique story of how they met, or more correctly, never met. They share the story of "the night they never met," with friends and family. It's a comedic tale and engenders much laughter each telling. He does not explain his side of the story until a year or so into their relationship. It is sweet and she cherishes it.

They dance in the kitchen to Frank and Neil, and struggle to adjust habits with long-grown roots. She bristles at him in her kitchen cooking space. He makes weird food, she thinks. He wants to help with the chores. "Please don't mow the grass or clean the garage," she pleads. "These are my reasons for getting out of bed. I am lost without them." He leaves feeling chastised and useless. He wants to take care of her; she is not a woman who allows herself to be cared for, only about. "Can I take out the trash?"

"Yes, okay." That is one task she is willing to give up.

"Happy Birthday," he says and hands her a pillowcase filled with gifts: plastic glasses with flower bases, a bottle of wine, pink flamingos and a cheese cutter. She is bewildered but acts enthused. This is the first time she has ever gotten a gift in a pillowcase. They are in a restaurant and she is feeling self-conscious. He does not notice. She buys him shirts and pants for his birthday wrapped in Hallmark paper.

She enters the bedroom to find him ironing his shirt.

"What are you doing?" she asks, astonished at the position of his shirt on the board.

"I'm ironing," he says a bit indignant. "What's wrong?"

"You're using the wrong end of the ironing board," she says and starts to chuckle.

"It works for me."

She realizes the world is set up for right-handed people and he is a lefty. Besides, the more she thinks about it the more she realizes the shirt actually fits better at the other end of the board. It doesn't matter though; her midwest brain will not let her use that end.

She writes him poems:

This Moment

Sleep glides by
my window

>   *in its silken, starlit nightshirt,*
> *You drift across*
>   *my dreams*
>   *in your only "for me" smile*
> *I stand breathless*
>   *beside you*
>   *waiting for this moment.*

They share these lines curled up on the couch or sitting at the campfire. He has never had someone write him poems; she has never had anyone who understood her need to write them. He encourages her; she absorbs his compliments like a plant in the desert after a thunder shower.

Sometimes they compose together, humorous ditties, one line at a time, side by each (a phrase she brought from the Midwest with her). They laugh and breathe each other in. Sometimes he weeps having read her pain. Slowly, she allows her wounds to surface, briefly, and lets him massage them, gently. He stands on the edge of the pool, she encourages him to jump in, she will catch him. He swims in the deep water now and then. A spectator in life, he struggles with participating; she picks him first on her team and hands him the bat. Play ball!

David, the architectural designer extraordinaire, sits at his desk and sketches dreams. They do not sell here; people of limited vision do not buy them. He draws boxes for them; they are happy, he is not. Occasionally, a client of color and noise hires him; his juices flow out onto the drawing board. They are happy; he is happy.

THEY GO FOR A WALK. David slows down to catch his breath and then resumes the walk. Another thirty feet and he stops again. It takes a while to get home. He guzzles some water and sits down.

"Remember we have Casey's baseball game tonight," his partner calls down from upstairs.

"What time?" he asks.

"Around seven."

As they climb the bleachers at the ballpark, David stops to ease the tightness and then moves up again.

"Are you okay?" she asks as she looks into his ashen face.

"Yes, I'm fine."

He rubs his chest a couple of times and settles in to watch the game. Casey's parents are good friends, so they accompany them for pizza after the game and then head home.

She awakens at five in the morning. David is not in bed. She heads downstairs to the living room where he is lying awake with fearful eyes.

"What's wrong?" she asks.

"I can't get this tightness in my chest to ease up. I used my nitro but it's still there."

She stiffens. "How long has this been going on?"

"Since yesterday, I suppose."

"Let's go," she says.

"Go where?" he asks.

"To the hospital, where else? Dr. Connelly told you that if the pain did not subside with nitro, then get to the hospital immediately."

They get dressed, climb in the truck and head to the hospital. The emergency department is deserted at this hour. After donning the open-backed gown he is wired for sound. Wires and electrodes are stuck all over him. Within minutes, the admitting forms are being signed and nurses buzz about.

"We're admitting you Mr. Hall. You've had a heart attack and you'll need a work-up to determine a plan of action."

The words do not quite sink in—he had had a what? Heart attack? How can that be?

Several days of decisions and tests result in a final verdict of coronary artery bypass surgery—too many and too much blockage, for any other procedure. David can not sleep the night before the procedure. He can only think about how they are going to hook him to a machine, stop his heart, fix it, and then kick start it again. He feels like an automobile going in for an engine replacement. Doctors and nurses all talk like mechanics: disconnect this, hook up that, new hoses, etc. Weird, very weird. He feels like some freak with purple lines drawn up and down his legs. That is where they will harvest the vein to be used in the bypass. Soon he is on the gurney, staring at ceiling tiles.

His sisters, girlfriend and her daughter sit in the waiting room. A few recliner chairs, a sofa, a TV and a coffee pot line the walls, anticipation and anxiety fills the spaces between. His girlfriend completes crossword puzzle after crossword puzzle to keep her mind busy. She estimates that two puzzles equal an hour. It will take twelve puzzles to get to the point where he should be off the machine. Another trip for coffee and bathroom should eat up some time. It takes fifteen minutes to get to the cafeteria and back. Again she calculates the number of trips it would take to reach the first hurdle. Other families come and go. The phone rings, it is not for them. Is that good news, she wonders? She walks outside to use her cell phone sending updates through the airwaves. Not much to report but it takes up time. The sisters do needlepoint and read. No gallows humor is exchanged; funny just doesn't find its way to this waiting room. Sorrow and joy enter and leave at will.

Six hours pass. They stare at the phone, willing it to ring and dreading its summoning. Finally, their combined anxieties must excite the wires and it rings. She jumps up. "Hello."

"Is this Mr. Hall's family?" asks the voice at the other end.

"Yes," his partner replies.

"This is Joanne, the OR nurse, just letting you know he's off the machine and everything is working fine. We'll be a few more hours but all looks well. We'll be taking him to recovery and a nurse will come get you when you may see him."

"Thank you," is all she can think to say.

She exhales audibly. Tears leak out and her hands shake as she hugs his sisters, telling them the good news. Her legs get wobbly so she sits and sobs into her hands. She always knew she loved him, she just did not know how much.

David's recovery is as expected; the first six months are difficult but gradually their lives return to pre-event status. The days, weeks and months go by and each one sees him gain strength. It's March and spring is popping out all over. David leaves a note on her desk on Tuesday to plan on a dinner date on Thursday evening.

On Thursday afternoon she hangs up the phone; she is now a member of the unemployed. She is both stunned and relieved; after twenty years she is burned out and ready for a change. She can't believe she finally did it.

David enters her office in the back of the house for the third time that afternoon. "Dinner is at seven o'clock at La France."

"Yes, I know. It's only five-thirty. Why are you pacing? I'll be in the shower by six. That's plenty of time. I just mutually parted company with Halifax, Inc. Just give me a few minutes to absorb this. It's a big change. I know I said I hated my job and that it was time to pursue another dream, but I'm overwhelmed by the reality."

"I know, sorry, I just don't want to be late."

"We won't be."

They arrive at the restaurant at seven o'clock. The maitre d leads them to their favorite table. A bottle of wine is delivered within moments of sitting down. After a few sips David excuses himself. The waiter appears and she gives him their orders. She continues to enjoy the wine while wondering what is taking David so long. Men don't typically take much time in the bathroom. Somewhere around ten to fifteen minutes later he reappears—in a tux! At the same time a waitress brings a dozen red roses in a vase and places them on the table. She stares at David until, like in cartoons, a light comes on. David takes her hand, unrolls a piece of paper and reads a poem to her. Her hands begin to shake. When the poem is complete, he rises, walks around the table, gets down on one knee, and opens a small black box. Tears begin to run down her cheeks.

"Margaret Mary Casey, will you marry me?"

Her arms enfold him as she repeats over and over, "Yes, yes, yes, I will marry you." Her hand shakes as he places the ring on her finger and pulls tissue from his pocket to dab at the mascara streaks under her eyes. A friend mysteriously appears with camera in hand and captures the moment. She realizes he carefully planned all this; no wonder he was a nervous wreck this afternoon. They eat the meal in a happy state of shock. As they exit the restaurant, he ushers her to the curb where a limousine awaits. He has thought of everything.

In bed that night he asks again. Do you, Maggie, take crazy old me to be your husband?

She whispers, "I do."

Interlude XVIII

"...Please move forward and face one another, take each others hands...

Do you, David, promise to always be there for Maggie, to be ever aware of her needs, to be a good partner, to share the good days and the bad, to look forward to new adventures and to hold her in your heart forever?"

David: I do.

"Do you, Maggie, promise to always be there for David, to be ever aware of his needs, to be a good partner, to share the good days and the bad, to look forward to new adventures and to hold him in your heart forever?"

Maggie: I do.

ABOUT THE AUTHOR

The author lives with her husband, David, and their crazy dog, Chloe, at the base of the Colorado Naitonal Monument in western Colorado. She derives inspiration from the towering red cliffs which stand sentinel aside Red Canyon. Ms. St. Onge has a Master's Degree from the University of Wisconsin–Milwaukee and after a twenty year career in research, she shifted gears and put pen to paper. What you hold in your hand is her first, but certainly, not her last attempt, at being a novelist.